His Muse, Her Addiction

A Novella By Mya

Copyright © 2021 Mya

Published independently by Author Mya. All rights reserved. This book is a work of fiction. Names, characters, places, and incidents either are the product of the author's imagination or are used fictitiously and are not to be construed as real. Any resemblance to actual persons, living or dead, business establishments, events, or locales or, is entirely coincidental.
No portion of this book may be used or reproduced in any manner whatsoever without written permission except in the case of brief quotations embodied in critical articles and reviews.

Contents

Title Page	
Copyright	
His Muse, Her Addiction	1
Synopsis	2
Note from Mya!	3
Disclaimer	4
One	5
Two	16
Three	24
Four	34
Five	43
Six	52
Seven	61
Eight	70
Nine	77
Ten	81
Books By This Author	91

His Muse, Her Addiction

A Novella by Mya

Synopsis

Mutualism – a relationship in which both species benefit. For Chelsea Chisolm and Calvin James, they fit together like the perfect jigsaw puzzle. Their relationship was far from simple, a complex romance filled with mental, emotional, and physical strains for the both of them.

For Calvin, Chelsea was the perfect pastime. She was the missing piece to his creative drought. Her presence inspired him to create his best work.

For Chelsea, life was a never-ending cycle of bad days. The only time she truly felt peace was in the presence of Calvin.

Together, they go through the trials and tribulations of falling in love and figuring out themselves.

Note from Mya!

Hello readers! I want to first and foremost thank you for buying/downloading my latest release. I have been on a hiatus for quite a while and still getting back into the groove of things when it comes to this writing stuff.

I am a new mom; navigating through that is an exciting experience. So, as you may notice, my books reflect new ideas and perspectives I didn't have before.

I hope you all see the growth in my writing, but most importantly, I hope you enjoy this new release!

With love,

Mya

Disclaimer

This book contains topics of abuse, sexual assault, and mental health issues such as depression. If any of the matters mentioned above trigger you, please read with caution.

Thank you.

One

Chelsea

Digging my nails into the smooth, brown skin on the back of his shoulder, I tilted my head slightly as I opened my mouth to let out an exclamation of passion.

"Damn, baby," He panted near my ear as he placed one of his hands against the headboard to get leverage for his powerful thrusts. It was almost as if he was doing push-ups into me. "You're so damn wet."

I responded with an incoherent grunt, not able to arrange sentences correctly. I was more focused on the way he filled me to my core with his throbbing length. The way his body fit mine so perfectly made me wish this moment would never end.

All of my problems disappeared behind these four walls. The red LED lights transforming the white walls into the perfect environment for pure sexual bliss. The shade of the lights intensified the orgasms we'd share. The lights with the added early-90s and 2000s R&B playing in the background set the perfect vibe every time the two of us linked. The lights, the music, and the incorporation of liquor and high-quality weed. How could I not want to experience this feeling every night? I knew I was falling in love. I knew that if things kept going like this, it could become quite detrimental for me.

Did I care?

Of course not.

I often self-sabotaged my love life. I settled for the bare minimum in all of my romantic endeavors because it felt as though I didn't deserve anything else for so long. If it were up to my previous situation-ships, I'd have the words cum dumpster tattooed across my slightly large forehead. That's how they treated me.

For years, men treated me as a sex toy and not an actual human being with feelings. My pleasure wasn't even considered most of the time I'd engage in sexual intercourse with a partner. They got their nut and went on about their business, leaving me to handle my nut and sleep alone in my bed.

I had settled for this treatment for years until I met Calvin. Calvin was the first man to put my pleasure before his. He was the first man to take his time and learn the intricacies of my body. He touched me, pleased me, and held me in ways that were so foreign, I craved it every chance I got.

I was addicted to him, and I never wanted this to end.

"I'm about to cum," I breathed out a soft voice, wanting my warning to go unheard so that he wouldn't adjust the way he pleased my body.

"Cum for me."

Those three words were magical. The power of that phrase sent my body into a convulsing mess. My walls clenched around

Calvin's length, and I held on for dear life as the pleasure began to overflow. I was in a state of euphoria as I rode out my climax. I was sweaty, sticky, and ready for more. The first orgasm only fueled my body into overdrive.

"Let me climb on top and ride that nut out for you." I requested once my breathing had leveled out.

Calvin looked down at me with pure lust in his eyes, causing my womanhood to throb with pleasure. Pleasing him, pleased me. We moved around the bed until he was lying on his back, and I was straddling his hips. I leaned down to press my lips against his.

One trait that made me so attracted to Calvin was how his lips were so plump and kissable. They complimented my own so perfectly that it was as if God put them on his face specifically for me to kiss. I looked down at him, taking in all of his features. His eyes were a dark brown that almost looked black. He had a chiseled face accompanied by a short, thick, moisturized beard, whether it be a result of his products or my bodily juices that constantly coated the coarse, brown hair. His hair was in long locs that fell down his back; most of the time, he had them twisted into intricate designs. Tonight was different; they were in a wild mess that resembled vines from the jungle. He was my personal Tarzan.

He was 6'3, muscular, with a bit of plumpness in the abdomen area. He had a few tattoos scattering his body, and I enjoyed tracing my tongue along the lines of them every chance I could get.

Calvin looked increasingly attractive under the red LED lights in my room. The way the lights enhanced his features and made every part of him even more mouthwateringly enticing.

"Stop playing with it."

Calvin's voice brought me back to the present, where I had been rubbing my clit with the head of his dick. I smirked, tilting my head to the side to look into his eyes. I licked my lips and planted my feet firmly on the bed before slowly sitting on his rock-hard length. The way it slid in so effortlessly caused us both to moan as my wetness engulfed his throbbing erection. Once he was entirely inside of me and I had my hands placed firmly on his chest, I began to move up and down, giving my hips a slight twist as I did so.

"Shit." He moaned lowly, placing his hands on my waist to guide me.

My knees popped, and that caused us both to chuckle. "Damn, I guess I don't have knees like Meg, but I'm a keep riding like I do." I repositioned myself to plant my knees firmly on the bed, and I moved my hips back and forth.

Every time I moved my hips, feeling him hit my spot had me holding back the inevitable orgasm that was nearing its peak like a dam waiting to burst. I knew which movements drove him the craziest, so I leaned back, placed my hands on his thighs, and moved my hips in the motion that resembled scooping ice cream out of the container. I gave my hips an extra twist as I'd grind on the stiff member. Calvin bit down on his bottom lip and closed his eyes. He folded his arms behind his head and let out a slow, deep breath. Through all of this, I could feel his body tense underneath me. I leaned in, placing my hands on his neck and giving a slight squeeze as I twerked on his dick. I moved my ass like jello, encouraging him to nut.

When he reached out and grabbed my neck, I knew that he was close. We rode out our orgasms together, the feeling so intense that my legs shook uncontrollably. I fell onto the bed beside him and caught my breath.

"Damn." We breathed out together.

"Pass me the blunt." I lit the blunt and looked up at the ceiling fan. I was utterly content with life. After a session of sex with Calvin, I wanted nothing more than to finish a blunt, listen to music, and just enjoy the company of my friend.

That's what Calvin was. My friend with benefits, lots and lots of benefits. He provided great sex, powerful orgasms, and companionship that I'd never had before. From the moment we started this, I knew I wouldn't get a relationship out of it. I knew it was strictly sex. He made that clear from the beginning, yet I couldn't control how my mind and body reacted when we were together.

I met Calvin a few months ago through an event hosted by a mutual friend.

Dressed to impress, I climbed out of my friend's Camaro. My body was glistening with hints of the glitter body lotion I applied to my skin before placing on my black dress. This dress hugged my curves perfectly, and I was ready to get into whatever trouble found me tonight. My wig was flat ironed and rested straight down my back, and I had a soft glam look going on with my makeup.

Stepping into the venue, I saw a room full of people dressed in their best after five attire. One of the bottle girls quickly handed me a glass of champagne, which I graciously accepted and chugged with a quickness.

It would take something much more vital to affect me in any way, but I was ready to enjoy my night, regardless.

"Chelsea! Tiana!" A familiar voice called out from near the bar, and Tiana and I turned towards the sound and locked eyes with Derrick. Derrick, Tiana, and I had all gone to college together freshmen year. Derrick had decided that college just wasn't for him, and he dropped out and opened up his own clothing business. He was doing great for himself, seeing as a year later he's hosting his pop-up shops and allowing other entrepreneurs and creatives the outlet to network and sell their products.

"This event looks amazing! I plan on supporting black businesses tonight!" Tiana commented as she gestured to the many booths and tables set up around the venue.

"I appreciate y'all coming out and supporting me, man. It means so much that y'all show up and show out at every event." Derrick pulled us into a tight group hug. I laughed softly.

"Of course, we're going to support your pinecone head-ass every chance we get! We've been cooler than the other side of the pillow for years now! Since freshmen year, I knew you two would be my forever friends and—"

"Here she goes with the sentimental shit," Derrick teased. "A simple 'That's what friends are for, D' would've sufficed."

Tiana laughed. "You two are a mess."

We finished another glass of champagne before Derrick escorted us around the venue, introducing us to different people. I was utterly in awe at the talent around the room, but my jaw had nearly dropped to the ground when we stopped in front of the most attractive man I'd ever laid eyes on. His entire presence captivated me. I took in his artwork and was impressed by the passion exerting from the canvas.

"Wow," I breathed, taking in the realistic painting of a young, black boy and his father. "This is beautiful."

"Just like you," He responded, taking me back for a second.

I cleared my throat and allowed a smirk to make its way onto my face. Tiana and Derrick knew from the look in my eyes that I was about to flirt with this man for the rest of the night.

"Calvin, this is my friend Chelsea. Chelsea, this is Calvin." Derrick quickly introduced us to each other. I held my hand out for a proper handshake, and he pulled it up to his lips and pressed gently against the back of my hand, swiping his thumb across my knuckles in the process.

Not to sound like a cliché woman in a romance novel, but I knew that the way my entire body tingled, that I had felt a spark between us. I wanted to talk to this man all night long.

"It's a pleasure to meet you," Calvin said after releasing my hand.

"Mmm," I responded.

"I want to get back to selling my art, but I was wondering if I could speak with you after the event?"

"Absolutely."

For the rest of the event, I anxiously awaited the alone time I'd get with Calvin. Would we talk all night until the sun came up and then make plans to see each other again? Or would we cut the small talk and go right to bed?

"Girl, you plan on going home with him, huh?" Tiana asked as we sat at the bar.

I shrugged. "If the feeling is mutual and we both want it, then yeah. I would enjoy going home with Calvin."

"Just be careful," Tiana warned.

I rolled my eyes. "Duh."

"Bitch, I'm just saying! You know how you can sometimes be. Be cautious about ol' dude." She responded. "Something about him just doesn't feel right to me."

"Yes, ma'am."

When the event was over, I waited at the bar for Calvin. After he finished cleaning up, he sauntered over to me and leaned against the bar. "I'm not even going to beat around the bush. I think you're beautiful as hell, and I want to get to know you."

"Get to know me, or exchange a few words and go straight to sex?" I countered.

"I'm not going to lie; I would love to get to know you and go back to your place as well." He shrugged.

"When was the last time you got tested?" I asked.

I was never afraid to ask a potential partner about their sexual status because grown people should be comfortable enough to share this information. If people are not comfortable sharing test results to STDs and STIs, they shouldn't be getting into bed with each other. I refuse to allow myself to lay in bed with someone who doesn't regularly get checkups if they are sexually active.

If a man gets defensive about getting tested for STDs, I know that that's not a man I want to engage with in sexual activities.

"Yeah, I got checked at the beginning of the month. I can show you my results if you want."

"That would be perfect; I'll show you mine as well."

We talked about all types of things, and I honestly enjoyed the casual, lighthearted conversation we were sharing. Tiana cut our conversation short when she called my cellphone. I had almost forgotten that we had carpooled to the event. I told her that I would be out shortly.

"I have to head back home, but the night doesn't have to end here," I spoke to him as soon as I hung up the phone.

He smiled. "I would love to keep the night going."

We exchanged numbers, and I left.

I took a long, hot shower when I got back to my apartment. I made sure my room was spotless, and my candles were burning. I had my 90s playlist playing softly in the background as I prepared myself for tonight. I was silky smooth and ready for whatever the night brought. I took a couple of shots of Hennessey and sparked my blunt to calm my nerves.

I always got nervous when it came to new sexual partners because I had terrible experiences in the past. It was always hit or miss when it came to sex. I was used to being the pleaser, and very rarely was the same energy reciprocated. I hoped that tonight would be different. I hoped that Calvin would take his time and put my sexual needs ahead of his, something that rarely happened in my life.

As soon as he arrived, we didn't exchange many words. I led him to my room; we got comfortable and let our bodies do the rest. I sat on the edge of the bed while he sat beside me.

"I'm not even going to lie to you; I'm high as giraffe pussy right now," I confessed.

Calvin laughed. "Oh, for real?"

"I'm borderline cross-faded, but I am well aware of my actions. I want you to know that I consent to whatever we're about to get into." I explained.

Calvin looked at me with curious eyes. "You're different."

"What do you mean?" I questioned, angling my head slightly to the left to give him my full attention.

"Most women aren't as socially conscious as you. You intrigue me."

"I hope that's a good thing."

"It is."

There was a comfortable silence. I licked my lips. "I've wanted to kiss you all night."

"Kiss me then."

That night, I was pleased several times. He had me in positions I never even knew I was flexible enough to be in. He made me squirt and climax so many times; I was surprised the amount of fluid I'd released didn't cause dehydration.

We continued to meet up from that night, and after almost five months of linking, I knew that I didn't want to do this with anyone else. I'd cut off all of my old partners and only wanted Calvin.

I was in too deep.

I may even be addicted.

Two

Calvin

"How long do I have to stay like this?" She asked, rolling her eyes.

I chuckled, watching her cute lips scrunch into a pout. "A few more minutes, baby. I'm finishing up now!"

"Yeah, yeah." She tilted her head and continued to look at me as she ate her bowl of ice cream. I memorized every curve, dip, and angle of her body. I tried to immortalize her onto the canvas in front of me.

I wanted to capture her beauty onto the ample space so that the world could see what I saw every night I spent with her.

Chelsea was a special woman. She brought out my best work when we were together. The day I met her, a spark ignited within me, and I knew that I wouldn't want to let her go. I tried to hold on to this special bond we shared for as long as I possibly could.

I treated her like a queen. I pleased her as she'd never been pleased before. Before she started messing with me, these other niggas didn't satisfy her like she deserved to be satisfied. I had pride in my bedroom abilities because I knew nobody could please a woman better than I could. I always had them wanting more.

"How do you expect me to sit still when you look so sexy painting right now? I'm resisting the urge to push you up against the wall and suck your—"

Before she could finish her inappropriate comment, I closed the distance between us and pressed my lips against hers. When

I look at Chelsea, all I see is beauty personified. Her skin was a smooth, sandy brown. She had dark brown hair with wild curls. Not to mention, she was thick in all the right places. When she smiles, she lights up the whole room, even with the cute, small gap protruding between her two front teeth. Her personality drew me in the most because she could make any and everybody smile and laugh or give her their full, undivided attention.

Since I laid my eyes on her, I knew that I wanted to get to know her. I knew that I wanted to see if she tasted as good as she looked. After I got that first taste, I wanted to taste her every chance I could get.

See, with Chelsea, we were upfront and open about all of our sexual desires. She would milk my dick dry without a second thought, and I would provide her with such intense pleasure that she wouldn't have the energy to do anything but exist after a night of sex with me. I was a man who put the woman's needs before my own. Nothing made my dick spring into action more than the pleasure-filled moans a woman would make when she was at my mercy in the bedroom.

"Let's see how many times I could make you cum," I challenged as I laid her back on the bed and spread her legs slowly. I looked down at her womanhood, my mouth watering with anticipation. I leaned down and gave a slow, teasing lick against her clit.

"Calvin, please," she moaned, her hands instinctively going to latch on to my dreads like muscle memory. She intertwined my hair with her fingers and closed her eyes as I began to devour her wetness. I sucked and flicked on her clit gently while rubbing circles along her entrance. I'd teasingly dip a finger inside between licks.

"Tell me what you want, baby," I instructed when I tilted my head slightly to glance at her.

"I want you to put it in." She panted, trying to control her shaking legs.

I nodded, ready for the next challenge. In the smoothest motion I could muster, I pulled down my boxers and began stroking my length as I continued to lick and finger the wetness between her legs. Her moans made my dick stand up like it was giving a patriotic salute. I was so glad that we both got tested regularly. She told me time and time again that she only wanted me and that I was the only man pleasing her. I rewarded her loyalty with leg shaking, back-breaking, mouthwatering sex every time she wanted it. The bonus for me was that I could slide into her with no condom. I could feel her wetness engulf me and feel the intricacies of her walls clasping and unclenching around my length.

"Damn, you're so wet." I had to bite down on my lip to calm my growing pleasure as I slid into her. I was a bit bigger than average, so it took time for her to adjust to my size. When she was ready, she gave me the okay to begin my strokes. I took pride in how I treated the pussy. There were many uneducated men out there who got all of their sexual knowledge from other ignorant men. Every pussy was different and should be treated as such. One woman might be more naturally wet than another, but that didn't make the other woman any less desirable. I also hated when men said that the pussy was so tight, which was basically them bragging about not arousing their partner correctly. The vagina expands when a woman is stimulated; the more turned on she is, the more comfortable it is to slide into it. Depending on the dick size and width, it would be easier for specific measures to enter the pussy better than others. Sex was more than just penetration. It was a complex process not too many people took time to figure out.

I started stroking in and out of her slowly, making sure to go balls deep with every thrust. After a few minutes of slow strokes, I changed the rhythm and tempo and lifted one of her legs onto my shoulder.

"Oh shit," She gasped as I began hitting a different spot inside of her. She spread her arms out and gripped the sheets. Her bowl of ice cream, long forgotten, began to melt beside us. I made a mental note of its placement on the bed because I did not want it spilling and causing an even bigger mess than what we were about to make.

I crossed her legs and pressed them against her chest. I pulled her to the edge of the bed and thrust into her. She couldn't run from the dick; her only option was to take it.

"I love this dick so much," she softly cried as she reached out for me. I smirked and closed the distance between us, continuing to pound into her but pressing my lips against hers. She used her tongue to open my mouth for a sloppy, passionate kiss. We tongued each other down while I continued to pound into her. We probably resembled wild rabbits the way we were humping and kissing so intensely.

"Whose pussy is this?" I asked, already knowing the answer.

She locked eyes with me, "yours." The way she said that one word so breathlessly with ease sent my body into overdrive.

"Turn over," I instructed.

She quickly moved onto her stomach. I watched her arch her back and licked my lips as her wetness came into view. I climbed onto the bed and inserted myself inside of her. She pressed her face into the mattress and began throwing her ass back. I slapped it encouragingly as I met her halfway.

"I'm about to c—"

"Hold that shit in, baby," I warned haphazardly.

She whined. "I can't."

I gripped a handful of her hair and pulled her head back, still pounding into her. "Cum on this dick."

She shook as she began to release her creamy orgasm all over my dick. I didn't stop until I neared my climax. I pulled out and rubbed the nut onto her ass. I let out a throaty groan before collapsing onto the bed beside her. She turned over and looked at me with lust-filled eyes.

"That was amazing," she commented.

I hummed in agreement. We laid in peaceful silence for a moment before we both headed to the restroom to clean up. We were comfortable with each other, so the after-sex clean-up was never awkward. Once we were both cleaned up, I pulled on a fresh pair of boxers while she pulled a matching bra and pantie set out of her bag. I went back to painting while she cleaned up the room. I appreciated the way we could enjoy each other's company. Most women I had encounters with would either be too chatty, too clingy, or obnoxiously awkward. Chelsea was different, and I genuinely enjoyed her presence.

As my painting started coming together, I got lost in the colors, angles, and shading. It was as if the world around me had disappeared, and the only thing on my mind was the complex image on the canvas. I loved getting caught up in a piece like this. I would be in this room until it was complete.

"I'm going to go ahead and head back to my house," Chelsea spoke into the air, bringing me out of my trance.

I nodded, not taking my eyes off of the painting. "A'ight, let me know when you make it home safely. I'll probably be here the rest of the night, but I'll respond when I take a break."

"Remember to eat." She reminded. "And stay hydrated."

"Yes ma'am, I will."

I liked that Chelsea cared about my health. I liked that she wanted me to be the best version of myself. I loved the fact that her presence unlocked a passion within me that produced some of my bestselling art pieces. Since meeting Chelsea, I'd made almost a 150% increase in sales. She supported my talents more than I did at times, and that was very inspirational to me. Every creative deserved a Chelsea in their life.

It was well into the early morning when I finally finished my painting and had put it on display to dry. I turned up the music and began cleaning the room. I had this studio where I conducted all of my work, equipped with a fully functioning kitchen and bathroom and a washer and dryer—everything I needed to sustain long sprints of work without the need to leave the studio. Once I had showered and put on a fresh outfit, I locked up the studio and made my way to my car. I headed back to my house and parked in the driveway.

When I walked in, silence greeted me, except for the sound of the air condition humming. I walked through the house and made my way down the hall to the bedroom. I undressed down to my boxers and climbed into bed. I wrapped my arm around the sleeping woman in the bed and soon joined her in slumber.

"Daddy!" The pressure of a toddler woke me up out of my sleep a few hours after I'd fallen into my slumber. I quickly moved my hands to grab the minor child and began tickling them.

"Who dares disturb the royal heinous in his slumber?!" I asked in a fake, deep royal accent.

"Me!" The little child who looked like the miniature version of myself screamed with joy.

"Now you must pay!" I sat up and tossed the toddler over my shoulder before standing up out of bed and lifting him into the air. I threw the child onto the bed and began attacking him with tickles. His laugh filled the air, and I smiled at the sight of his excitement.

"Calvin! CJ! Breakfast is ready!"

His mother's voice brought us out of our tickle war. I swooped him up into my arms, and we walked into the bathroom. I sat him on the counter, and we washed our hands and faces then brushed our teeth. I slid on some sweatpants before allowing the child to climb onto my back. I carried him into the dining room, where his mother sat waiting for us.

I know there might be slight confusion about my current living situation. I lived in a home with my fiancée, Candace, and son, Calvin Junior. She was currently eight months pregnant and could pop any moment. I may sound like a horrible person, but I do not think that what I am doing is wrong. I provide for my family and never thought about stepping out until I met Chelsea. There was just something about her that intrigued me. I had initially planned to appease my curiosity, only to find myself wanting more of Chelsea as time continued. She unlocked something special inside of me that Candance never had.

Would I confess? No. I didn't love Chelsea; I just enjoyed the time we spent together. I loved my fiancée and had already decided that I would end things with Chelsea once the baby arrived. I figured this would just be something I took to the grave with me because I loved Candace and Calvin Junior and didn't want to lose my family because of my infidelities. It was pretty fucked up, but as long as nobody knew, nobody could get hurt.

"Breakfast tastes delicious," I commented as I dug my fork into the pancakes, sausage, and eggs on my plate.

"Thank you, honey."

I looked at my fiancée, and I smiled. She was everything a man could dream of and more. She was beautiful, independent, and had the perfect ass-to-titty ratio. Her skin was a smooth, golden brown that she put in damn near hours of skincare to maintain. Her hair was thick and black, but she kept her hair protected with wigs and braids most of the time. She currently rocked a honey brown wig that looked like those classic wet and wavy styles. Before I got her pregnant, she was a model. She had done commercials, magazine spreads, runway shows, and more. Given the opportunity of painting her for one of my commissions, we clicked immediately. Before I knew it, she was pregnant with Junior, and we were moving into our home. I proposed to her a year into us living together. We'd been delaying planning our wedding for one reason or another. I knew she wanted something extravagant, so I was saving up to make sure she got whatever she wanted. It would just take some time.

"What do you have planned for today?" Candace questioned as she collected our breakfast dishes.

"I wanted to take the day off and relax around the house because I have an event this weekend. I want to take a self-care day to get my mind in the right state to sell some artwork." I explained.

She hummed in acknowledgment. "Lazy day around the house? Want to watch movies and eat junk food?"

"I'd love that."

She pressed her lips against mine and smiled. "I miss you."

I almost felt bad for being out of the house so much. However, I did my job as a fiancé and baby father. I took good care of Candace and ensured her comfort. I made sure that I was a call away in case she needed her cravings met or attention. Luckily for me, during this third trimester, all she does is sleep and have her sister, Haley, watch Junior during the days when she's too tired to care for him herself.

"I miss you too. I promise I'm going to get better at navigating my work and home schedule." I was serious about that. As soon as she popped our baby girl out, I'd cut ties with Chelsea and make Candace my main priority again. I felt as though this was a fool-proof plan. Chelsea knew there wouldn't be more to our arrangement. It was apparent in the beginning that this was strictly for pleasure purposes. I just pray that she understands when the time comes. I'd hate to break her heart once all of this is said and done.

Three

Chelsea

Growing up, I was an only child. I would visit cousins here and there, but overall, I stuck to myself. I was fortunate enough to be raised by both parents. Although they worked most of the time, most people would categorize me as a latchkey kid. I'd come home from school and have to fend for myself until late in the evening when they'd return home. Some kids in my situation would use that opportunity to get into trouble. I was different.

I was the type of kid who would get lost in books, take naps, and do my homework, no matter if I had adult supervision or not. I didn't have many friends because I'd instead find solitude through the adventures and storylines of the books I read than go out and socialize with people.

However, the shy girl I was as a child grew into a party animal in college. I began drinking and smoking the first day of my freshmen year in college. Since that day, I don't think I've genuinely been sober. I don't believe I had a problem because I knew my limits and could stop whenever I deemed fit. I didn't depend on the substances to get me lit or fix any of my problems. I just enjoyed the feeling I got when I was under the influence.

Not many people know that I suffer from depression. I have moments in my life where I feel as though the world would be a better place if I weren't taking up space. I have moments when I cry myself to sleep because the slightest inconvenience ruined my whole mood. I struggle with keeping a smile on my face, feeling beautiful and loving myself, and staying alive.

I don't share these feelings and thoughts with people anymore because I was called an attention seeker and told to get over it the one time I did share. People told me to pray my depression away and find the good in things, and everything would get better. But it's been almost five years, and I am still struggling with my mental health each day. I was a firm believer in God and made sure to have a spiritual relationship with him. I'd read my Bible and interpret the word how I felt it was necessary. Still, I despised religion due to the hypocritical Christians who threw the Bible at you and expected you to blindly follow the Bible. I was content with knowing God my way without the "holier than thou" mindset some Christians had. I also didn't think that prayer was the answer to everything. Prayer without action was pointless, in my opinion. I could pray all day, but if I did nothing to align myself with the prayers I was doing, it would all be a waste of time. I couldn't pray away my depression. I needed to seek therapy, but I couldn't afford that, nor was I ready to face those demons. I would continue to do my drugs and alcohol and partake in mind-blowing sex as my coping mechanisms.

For a long time, I used sex as my outlet to deal with my problems. I knew that those few minutes sharing such an intimate action with someone else would give me a brief moment of happiness and comfort, even though right after, I'd feel like shit again. The temporary pleasure only sent me deeper into my periods of self-loathing and disappointment. I knew what I was doing was unhealthy, but I did not have enough care to change.

If it weren't for Tiana and Derrick, there's no telling where I would be in life right now. They knew that I struggled with my mental health and made sure to check in on me every once in a while, especially if they hadn't heard from me.

It had been a few weeks since the last time we hung out

together, and we'd finally found the time in our busy schedules to link for brunch.

"You look beautiful!" Tiana complimented me as I got out of my car. We embraced each other in a tight hug and admired each other's looks for the occasion.

"Me?! Girl, have you seen YOU?!" I asked, holding her hand up and instructing her to do a spin. I licked my lips and hummed in admiration. "T baby, you are a goddess!"

"If only we were gay, we could run off and get married. I'd be the luckiest woman in the world to wake up next to your fine ass every morning!"

"Can you two shut the hell up and come on?" Derrick asked, interrupting our compliment war. We laughed heartily and made our way into the restaurant. Once we were seated and had our orders taken, we jumped right into catching up with each other.

"So, I finally found a hospital to begin my residency," Tiana began.

"That's amazing!" I cheered.

Derrick agreed. "Oh, we have to celebrate this weekend! I'll bring the Henny!"

"Y'all know Henny goes straight to my coochie," I reminded, halfway teasingly.

Tiana chuckled. "Bitch, everything goes straight to your coochie!"

"Fuck you!"

We all laughed together. I cherished these moments with my friends. Being able to enjoy each others' presence was all I needed to keep pushing through my hard days.

"For me, sales have been steady. I have another pop-up shop scheduled for next month, so I'm finalizing everything now. I think I'm going to propose to Natalie—"

Tiana and I gasped in unison. "WHAT?!"

"I am in love with that girl. She's the best thing in my life, and I want to take it to the next level." Derrick explained. I can hear the genuineness in his voice.

"I'm so happy for you," Tiana was smiling from ear to ear.

I looked at Derrick intently before I made my comment. "This is a big commitment. Are you sure you're ready for this?" Derrick had only known Natalie for a few months. I felt as though this was kind of sudden.

"No offense, but you've never actually been in a relationship, so you really can't comment on mine." Derrick's smile morphed into a scowl, and I knew that I'd ruined the entire vibe at the table.

"D, I didn't mean to offend you. I'm just saying; you've only known the girl a few months. Marriage is a huge step." I tried to reword my feelings in a more understanding way.

Derrick shook his head. "When you can get a nigga to take you seriously, then you can talk to me. Until then, don't offer me any relationship advice."

"Heard." I didn't feel like arguing, so I dropped the subject entirely. It was no use in reasoning with Derrick, especially when he would dismiss anything I said. He was borderline about to hurt my feelings, so to spare us both, I decided not to keep pushing my point.

I wasn't wrong, though. Derrick shouldn't be rushing into marrying Natalie when the two of them barely knew each other. Regardless of my relationship history, my opinions on relationships are still valid. No one should jump into marriage blindly, especially since Derrick and Natalie haven't lived together yet. They only see each other in the fairytale light. When in reality, until you've experienced a person in all of their forms, you should not rush into marriage with them. People could be marrying the Devil reincarnated and wouldn't even know because they judge the person off of one form.

People are multifaceted. We are constantly evolving; who I was last month does not accurately represent who I am today. I'm always learning, changing, and growing from every experience that I have, which is why I believe no one should get married until they've seen the person they are dating in every season.

"But, what's new with you?" Tiana asked to help release some of the tension in the air.

I shrugged. "Nothing new, really. I'm still working at the firm, still getting astronomically high, and still sleeping most of my days away."

"No new boo?" She questioned.

I shook my head. "Nope. Casual sex here and there, that's all." I easily lied. I didn't need Tiana and Derrick judging me for my sneaky links with Calvin. What Calvin and I had was fine the way it was, with no one knowing what we were doing. I knew they would disapprove of our relationship—situationship because it was very complicated. He didn't take me on dates or hang out with me as friends. We were strictly involved in the sexual benefits.

"Casual sex is cool, long as you're putting yourself first and staying safe," Tiana added.

I nodded. "Always. You know I'm always safe."

Brunch went uneventful after that. We ate in comfortable silence with the occasional short conversation. I had enjoyed my bottomless mimosas to the point where I was feeling great. I wanted nothing more than to go home, soak in the tub and invite Calvin over for some hot sex.

"Until next time!" We said our goodbyes, though I made sure to hug Derrick. We may have had our disagreements, but we never wanted to leave on a sour note at the end of the day. I know he may have said some hurtful things in the heat of the moment, but I knew he didn't mean to hurt my feelings. His defense mechanism when he felt attacked was to attack back.

When I pulled off onto the main street, I called Calvin. The call went to voicemail. I tried one more time, but that call went straight to voicemail without a ring. I figured he'd been busy with painting, so I sent him a text inviting him over for the night. I got back home and immediately undressed and hopped in the shower after I'd lit a few candles and lit a blunt, of course. I relaxed in my hot bubble bath and scrolled aimlessly on my phone, bouncing between apps as I did so.

"Maybe I should get a cat or dog," I said out into the quiet room. "A little companion to keep me company during my lonely days."

One thing about me, I knew for a fact that I didn't want to have kids. I was already barely holding on to my sanity; adding the stress of bringing a child into this world would probably be the last straw to break me fully. Pregnancy is a crazy experience with hormonal changes and then the process of giving birth, the pain of that mixed with another wave of hormonal changes... My mental state would take a hit that I would never recover from if I were to get pregnant.

I commend those women who can go through this once or several times. I could not and will not ever. I never missed a day of my birth control, and I planned on getting my tubes tied soon too. I was serious about this choice. I'd probably end up single for the rest of my life because I'm not sure I'd be able to find a man who could respect this choice.

When I finished my bath, I dried off. I slid on my robe and did my skincare routine before taking my bottle of wine and blunt into the living room and sitting in my recliner. I kicked my feet up, turned on a movie, and welcomed peace.

Sometimes, I was content with my own company. Sometimes, I can fight the urge to get lost in my evil thoughts. Tonight, I was winning. Tonight, I was content and at peace. I enjoyed my wine and blunt and this rom-com on Netflix when my phone dinged, catching my full attention. I picked up the iPhone and smiled when I saw Calvin's name in my notifications. The smile immediately fell into a slight frown when I read his text message, though: **We need to talk.** Those four words are the epitome of anxiety. The dread that filled me from head to toe was almost demobilizing as I stared at the message thread, wondering how I was supposed to respond.

My mind was racing. What could have possibly happened from the last time we linked to now? What could have possibly warranted the need to engage in conversation that didn't end in my mouth around his dick or me riding him like a cowgirl riding a horse at the rodeo?

When I finally built up the courage to respond, I simply said okay and waited for his response. My phone dinged shortly after, and it felt like my heart was about to explode through my chest. I read his text: **I'll come over tonight. I'll see you in about 30 to 40 minutes.**

I liked his message and put my phone down. A million thoughts began to bombard my mind as I thought about the last few moments we'd share. I couldn't recall a time where I had done something wrong. I couldn't remember a time when he'd done something wrong. The last few times we'd spent together was filled with laughs, smiles, and plenty of sex. This sudden change in his character caught me off guard to the point I was about to have a panic attack.

"Calm down, Chels, calm down."

I went into my stash and pearled another blunt. Instead of wine, I decided tonight would be best if I drank the Hennessey as a substitute. I took three shots back-to-back with no chaser and then lit my blunt. I walked into my bedroom and lit some candles and incense to fill the air. I turned on the blue LED lights and laid down. I finished the blunt and was as high as alien pussy. My eyes were so low that I probably wouldn't have known they were open if I didn't feel myself blink. My whole body felt sensitive, and I was now ready for whatever bomb Calvin came and dropped on me.

As I began to doze off, my phone ringing woke me up. I answered it without really paying attention to the caller ID, but I already knew who it was.

"I'm outside."

"Okay."

I went down the hall to the front door and opened it lazily. He walked in and made his way down the hall to my bedroom. I followed behind after locking the door. When we both got into the room, we sat on the bed, and he looked at me.

"We have to end these links."

"Okay."

"That's it?" He questioned.

"Did you come over here to tell me something that you could have sent in a text? Or did you come over here so we could fuck one last time?" I asked. When the high wore off, I knew the devastation would settle in because of the words he spoke, but I'd continue my calm approach for now. I couldn't let him see me upset over him ending things.

Calvin rubbed his hands down his face and shrugged. "I don't know why I'm here, Chels. I honestly could have done this shit over text, but I wanted to see you."

"Let's quit the lying. You don't have to care about my feelings. You're not feeling me and our current arrangement anymore. We can fuck, and you can leave me like everybody else. It's cool." I shrugged.

"Chels—"

"Enough. Don't blow my high with any more talk. We fucking or not?" I asked.

Calvin looked at me with an unreadable expression. He was most likely analyzing my responses, but doing so was actually pointless. Calvin no longer wanted relations with me. Our sneaky links would come to an end now that he no longer wanted to continue with our current arrangements.

"You right. C'mere." He pulled me onto his lap and looked me deep in the eyes. I tilted my head to the side and placed my hands on his shoulders. As I rubbed at his neck softly, I looked at him. I was hurt, but for now, I would just enjoy the last moment I'd share with him.

I pressed my lips against his, slowly. I slid my tongue along his bottom lip, and he parted the plump, soft skin to allow my tongue access. When my tongue made contact with his, things began to pick up. He rubbed my body soothingly yet firmly as if he was trying to memorize every curve of my body one last time.

"Lay down." Calvin's bold, masculine voice filled the room, causing intense chills to travel down my spine. I moved off of his lap and crawled onto the bed, resting my head on the pillow.

I looked up at him as he stood up and stripped down to his boxers. His body was perfection. Everything about him turned me on, and I was ready for our last moments together. He turned my LED lights to red and licked his lips as he made his way over to me. He pulled my legs down to the edge of the bed and spread them wide. I was a wet, throbbing mess as he slid his tongue along the crease of my lips. My body jolted and squirmed as he flicked his tongue against my clit. I instinctively placed my hands on top of his head and tangled my fingers through his hair. This would be the last time I got to spend with my Tarzan.

He slid two fingers inside of me and repeatedly did the "come here" motion until I was squirting my juices against his beard. He moved his head from between my legs, and I leaned up to pull him into a kiss, tasting myself on his lips. He tongue kissed me while we got into our first position. He stroked himself a few times and began rubbing the head of his length against my moist, throbbing entrance. He rubbed teasingly slow, causing me to whimper with anticipation. I placed my hands on his shoulders as he slowly inserted himself inside of me.

The way he filled me to my core was the best feeling in the

world. The way our bodies fit so perfectly against each other, it felt as if he was supposed to be the man I'd marry.

As he stroked in and out of me, I could feel the tears pooling in the back of my eyes. I closed my eyes and pulled him closer, breathing in his scent. I held on for dear life as he slowly but powerfully thrust into my entrance. "Please, don't stop." I cried into his ear, making sure to brush my lips against his earlobe. He placed one hand on my headboard and the other around my waist. He stretched a bit before adjusting his angle and digging into me deeply.

"Damn, you're so wet." He grunted through clenched teeth, continuing his powerful thrusts.

"Only for you," I responded, which was true. Nobody else got the pleasure of fucking me the way Calvin had. I wouldn't even want anybody else touching me because I knew they wouldn't be able to satisfy me as Calvin does.

"Fuck, I'm finna cum—"

"Please don't. I don't want this to end." I could feel the tears falling down my face. This was it. He'd nut, and I'd never see him again. I'd be left here alone, like every other time.

"I can't hold on—" He pulled out and nutted on my stomach. He fell on the side of me and looked up at the ceiling while he caught his breath.

It was over now.

Four

Calvin

As I watched the tears slide down her face, regret immediately overtook me. My intentions were never to hurt her. I assumed we'd both been on the same page this entire time. I had fucked up. Watching her cry like this, I wasn't sure what to do at this moment. Do I reach out and wipe her tears, apologize, or do we continue to have sex?

We cleaned up from the first round, but I wasn't ready to leave just yet. I wanted to end things on a positive note. I tried to put a satisfied smile on Chelsea's face before we cut ties forever. It may have caught Chelsea off guard, but she had to have known this wasn't going to last forever. When we talked about families and long-term goals, we didn't see eye to eye. She didn't want kids, yet I was about to have my second child any day now. She didn't have the same outlook on life as I did. We weren't as compatible as I initially thought, but the sex was always enough to ignore those differences, especially since I didn't plan on ever getting serious with her.

Now, as we lay there together, I was overcome with guilt. The sadness in Chelsea's eyes was enough to make me want to figure out a way to keep fucking her while taking care of my family... I knew that was never going to be a real option. If Candace ever found out about this, she'd pack up and leave me without a second thought. I couldn't lose her and my kids. Chelsea would just have to move on.

"I'm sorry," I finally broke the silence that had filled the air.

Chelsea shrugged, lighting a blunt. "This wouldn't be the first time, and probably won't be the last time that this will happen to me. I'm never the final choice. I'm always the pastime woman. Niggas love to fuck on me until they're ready to settle down, then I'm tossed to the side like an old gaming console so that he can go and connect with the latest trend."

"It's not like that at all—"

"You said it yourself that nobody has ever inspired you to create such powerful paintings. You said that I unlocked a side of your artistic abilities you didn't even know you possessed yourself. Now that you've been able to continue to produce those quality art pieces, you don't need me anymore. You'll go and find your forever woman, and I'm left behind… as always. It's okay, though. I've accepted my fate, knowing that I'm not lovable. I'm not the woman any man would choose to settle down with because I'm broken and used goods." Chelsea was saying some heavy stuff, yet her tone of voice was monotone and emotionless. It was as if she'd lost all hope, and I was the cause of this epiphany.

I turned her head to look at me. She blew smoke out of her nose and dumped the ashes on the ashtray before finally giving me her attention. Her eyes were red and puffy, most likely due to the combination of crying and smoking. I stroked her cheek with my thumb and sighed heavily. "You are not the problem. You've been great to me this whole time, but I have been living a double life and doing things I had no business doing in the first place. If we had met in different circumstances, you'd be the perfect girl for me. It's just that I have other responsibilities that require my undivided attention moving forward, and I wouldn't be able to do that with you around."

"You don't owe me any apologies or explanations."

"But I do."

Chelsea shook her head. "Listen, you've done enough. We've

fucked one last time; you honestly can get dressed and leave. I don't need you to stay to lull me out of the saddened state you caused. It's counterproductive."

"I don't want to lea—"

"Calvin, please stop." Chelsea shook her head and shifted on the bed to get comfortable. "You may not be used to the whole fuck and dip concept, but you're literally doing it wrong."

"The plan wasn't to fuck and dip. I honestly cherished everything we did over the past few months."

"Almost six." Chelsea tossed in.

"Huh?"

"You said the last few months like we haven't been doing this for almost half a year!"

"I just have to get back to reality, and what we were doing wasn't aligning with my plans." I tried to explain.

"The way you're still here…" Chelsea looked at me with an unreadable expression. I knew she was trying to piece together the missing explanations of my words. "You've had a girlfriend this entire time, huh?"

My eyes widened. "How did—"

"Get out, please." Her voice cracked, and I could tell from the way she kept blinking and rubbing her eyes that she was crying. I reached out, which caused her to pull away from me immediately. "Calvin, get out. Go home to your happy family. She probably has kids too, huh?"

"I have a son, and she's due to deliver my daughter any day now."

"Yup, you've managed to blow my high now completely. Have a great life, and I wish your girl a safe delivery. Now please get out."

"Okay."

I stood up, grabbed my belongings, and headed to the front door. Chelsea followed me shortly after and stood at the entrance. I looked at her, sadness present from her body language to her facial expressions.

"I really didn't mean to cause you any harm. My actions are all a reflection of my character. In no way, shape, or form does this define you as a woman. I wasn't upfront about my intentions and took advantage of our arrangement. I apologize for any pain I may be causing you," I didn't want us to end on such a sore note. I know that this could be a terrible situation from her perspective, but I wanted to make it better.

"Honestly, fuck you. I hope your girlfriend finds out and dumps your sorry ass. You are truly scum. I can't believe I thought I was in love with you. Fuck you, and delete my fucking number." It was as if someone flipped a switch, and Chelsea completely snapped. She slammed the door in my face after pushing me out of her home.

Hearing the door slam made me feel like complete shit. I misread Chelsea, which caused her so much pain. I thought she was cool with our arrangements, but to hear her say that she had fallen in love with me was a shock. I was blindly hurting her while using her for my benefit and pleasure.

I forgot that everybody couldn't handle casual sex without feelings of getting involved. I could have hot, passionate sex with someone for years and never catch feelings. People didn't have the skills to differentiate their lustful feelings from the sense of true love. For some people, a few minutes of mind-blowing sex could make them fall deeply in lust with someone. I honestly don't think anyone who falls in love through sex is genuinely in love. They may be in-lust, but I doubt they were actually in love. Love was more than a physical connection. Love was a complex feeling that came from experiencing life with someone. I'd never even spoken to Chelsea outside of the bedroom, excluding meeting her at the popup shop when we first met.

The entire ride home, I thought about Chelsea and how she reacted to me ending things and telling her about the family I had. I felt like complete shit, but I should have known that it would be like this. I kept that information from her. I allowed her to think she was the only woman in my life, even though the signs were there. What woman would fall in love with a man she only saw when he wanted sex? I'd never taken her out on an actual date or anything.

When I got home, I took another shower, brushed my teeth, washed my face, and pulled on a pair of boxers. Climbing into bed, I draped my arm over Candace's belly and rubbed soothing circles on the round bump. She snuggled closer to me, and I kissed the back of her neck. I fell asleep almost immediately after.

The bedroom door slowly creaked open, causing my senses to go into overdrive and the hair on my body to stand tall. I didn't move immediately; instead, I listened for their footsteps.

Why the hell was I acting so scared? This was my house. Whoever dared to come into my home and harm my family would be dealt with accordingly.

I sat up in bed and looked at the intruder.

"Chelsea?"

"You thought I was going to let this shit go without a fight?" She quizzed, folding her arms across her chest. "Right game, wrong bitch."

"Please don't do this. I love my fiancée."

"Did you love your fiancée when you were balls deep in this pussy every other night?! Did you love your fiancée when you approached me on some flirting shit and came back to my house?" She interrogated me, throwing out questions at rapid speed.

"I know you're hurting—"

"You couldn't even begin to fathom the degree of anger I am right now. I thought you were different, but you're just like the rest of 'em. Selfish." She began to grow angrier. Her body language was becoming defensive.

I stood up from the bed and walked over to her. I reached out to hold her hand, but she snatched away from me. "What do you want me to do?" I asked.

"I want you to confess to your lil fiancée about what you've been doing behind her back. I want her to know the filthy, lying, cheating man she's about to marry and have another child with hasn't been faithful. She deserves to have the choice of choosing whether to be with you or not."

My eyes widened at her demand. I shook my head. There was no way in hell I would do something like that. I would take this sin to the grave with me. I loved Candace and CJ with all my heart and didn't want to lose them over a minor fling. "I can't do that."

"You can't? Or you won't?"

"Both."

She laughed, a laugh so sinister that it sent chills down my spine. She pulled out her phone. After scrolling for a short time, she tapped the screen a few times and then smirked. "You didn't want to handle the situation like a real man, so I handled it for you. I just sent your little fiancée a message with one of our sex tapes attached."

My heart felt as if it had fallen out of my ass. I felt my whole world crumble to pieces.

How could I have been foolish enough to allow her to record our sexual endeavors? That was honestly a rookie mistake on my part.

"You fucking bitch!" I shouted out in anger.

"I wasn't a bitch when you would pin me to the bed and drop dick inside of me, now was I?" She still had this wicked smirk on her face which angered me like no other. I lunged for her as the bedroom door opened for a second time.

Standing in the door was Candace with her phone hanging loosely between her fingers. "What is this, Calvin?" Her voice cracked, *and I felt like the worst man on Earth.*

"Baby—"

"He's been fucking me for months, sis. While you're pregnant, going through changes, and dealing with one of the most life-threatening yet beautiful experiences a woman could go through, he's been dicking me down and slutting me out several times a week." Chelsea spoke directly to Candace.

I resembled a deer in headlights until something in me snapped. I reached out and wrapped my hands around Chelsea's throat. I squeezed, yet the harder my grip got, the louder she laughed.

"Shut up! Shut up! Shut up!" I kept repeating as I choked her.

"You're getting everything you deserve."

Jumping up into a sitting position, I woke up out of my sleep. My head was pounding severely. After I wiped at the tiny beads of sweat that had accumulated on my forehead, I stood up from the bed.

"Are you okay?" Candace's voice caught me off guard, causing me to twitch.

I nodded, walking into the bathroom. "Yeah."

"You were screaming in your sleep. What were you dreaming about?" She asked from in the bedroom.

"I can't remember," I lied smoothly.

She hummed. "I didn't feel like cooking this morning, but I and CJ had cereal."

"I'm not hungry, so it's cool," I replied. I took care of my morning routine and then stepped into the closet to get dressed. After I'd put on a comfortable fit, I walked back into the bedroom and sat next to Candace on the bed. "How are you feeling?"

"Tired. I don't have any strength to do anything anymore. I just want to sleep until the baby arrives."

I rubbed her stomach soothingly. "What did the doctor say

at the last visit?"

"Any day now. Whenever Cierra is ready to make her debut, we'll be ready."

"Absolutely. I love you so much." I kissed her lips. "I thought that after Cierra is born, we'd go ahead and schedule the wedding for next summer?"

She gasped. "Really?!"

"Yes, I want to stop procrastinating. Tomorrow isn't promised, and I don't want to spend too much longer without you sharing my last name." I said honestly.

If I was indeed done playing in the streets, then it was time to make things official for real. Candace deserved a faithful husband, and that's what I would be for her from this day forward. I just had to take care of a few things first.

"Do you have to go to work today?" She asked.

I shook my head. "I can go set up shop later. Want to have another movie day?"

"Yes, please."

"I'll go check on CJ and get snacks. You get our movie lineup ready."

"Yes sir." She kissed my lips. I could see the happy shimmer in her eyes, and that honestly made me feel even more like shit.

As I walked out of the bedroom, I pulled out my cellphone and sent a text message to Chelsea. The statement read: **Hey, did you delete those videos we made?**

A few moments later, I received a response that made me sick to my stomach. **You need to come delete them yourself.** A few winking emojis followed the text.

She was playing games with me, and I knew that if I didn't nip this shit in the bud immediately, she'd keep testing her luck. I told her I'd come by tomorrow. After that, I called one of my cousins.

"Wassup cus?"

"You and Ray-Ray trying to make a quick hundred?" I asked as soon as my cousin Day Day answered the phone.

"Shit wassup?"

I told him what I wanted, and he agreed readily. I sent him the details and put my phone away. I'd never hurt a woman, but I wasn't about to play cat and mouse with a bitch. She'd learn to move on after this.

Five

Chelsea

Flick! Flick! Flick!

"Stupid ass lighter!" I shouted angrily into the empty room.

After attempting to light my blunt for a whole minute, I stood up from my lying position in bed to grab another lighter. When I successfully brought a stable flame to the perfectly rolled cigarillo, I climbed back into bed and turned up the music.

It'd been only a few days since the Calvin situation, but I'd felt numb the entire time. To protect me from the intrusive thoughts of being unworthy of true happiness, I'd smoke a blunt almost every few hours to keep my head in the clouds.

How could I fall for the same lies every time? How could I allow yet another man to come into my life and use me until he got tired of me?

"I need to get out of the house," I said to myself. I texted my group chat that consisted of Tiana and Derrick and asked when we could all link again. Derrick told me about a pop-up shop he was hosting this weekend, and I knew I'd be there.

I'd put myself into a weed coma and was out soon after making plans with my friends. It felt as though I had hibernated because I didn't even remember falling asleep. All I know is the sound of glass breaking down the hall woke me out of my slumber. I immediately sprung out of bed when I'd registered what was going on.

I didn't have much, but I valued everything I owned. I worked hard for everything in my life, and for someone to feel comfortable enough to try to steal from me was shocking. So, for someone to feel the need to rob me was baffling. I lived in an ordinary neighborhood. It wasn't even like I lived in an extravagant upper-class environment either. This was shocking.

As I contemplated life, the bedroom door burst open, and suddenly I resembled a deer in headlights. I put my hands up in surrender. "Please don't hurt me," I whimpered out.

Everything in my home was replaceable except my life. I didn't react fast enough to grab my handgun in the safe. I honestly never thought I'd need it, but here I was put in a predicament that warranted protection. Unluckily, I had thought of the gun too late. Would I have even been able to actually pull the trigger? Probably not.

"Where are all your electronics?" One of the masked men asked.

I pointed to the corner. The two men grabbed my phone, laptop, tablet, and apple watch. I didn't argue or protest, seeing as the man in front of me had a gun pointed at me.

"Unlock your cellphone."

I did what they instructed and watched as the man scrolled through my phone for a few seconds before tapping a couple of times, and then he handed it back to me.

"You got some cute pictures on yo camera roll," One of the robbers complimented. "I see why my cousin was fucking witchu—"

"Nigga?!"

"What?"

"Let's go before she starts connecting dots." The two of them left with my electronics, and silence soon followed me.

I grabbed my phone and called the police before I facetimed

my friends. Adrenaline was still pumping through my veins, making it hard for me to fully process what had happened.

"Wassup Chels?" Tiana asked as soon as she answered the call.

"Damn, this must be serious if you are calling this late at night." Derrick skipped a greeting and went straight to commentary.

"I was just robbed at gunpoint. I called the police. Now I'm just waiting for them to come so I can file a police report," I explained as short and concisely as possible.

Derrick and Tiana had identical faces of disbelief. "Who would rob you?"

"I don't even know, but they took my laptop, apple watch, and tablet."

"Are you going to be okay to stay by yourself tonight?" Derrick questioned.

I nodded. "Yeah, I should be fine. They didn't hurt me or anything."

"Keep us updated on everything that's going on," Tiana instructed before we concluded the call.

By the time the police came and went, the sun had made its way high into the sky. I was utterly drained and wanted nothing more than to sleep the day away. Knowing that I wouldn't be able to sit through a day of work, I called my boss and told him what happened. He kindly gave me a few days off to relax and rest after going through that traumatic experience. I did just that.

When I finally woke up from my hibernation, I had many notifications waiting for me on my phone. I wasn't in the mood to converse with anyone, so I simply cleared the messages and sat up in bed. I stretched and rolled my head against my shoulders before I stood up and went into the bathroom.

I was robbed at gunpoint last night.

That thought alone made me lose control of my legs, but luckily, I caught myself before I could fall.

This neighborhood wasn't prone to crimes like this, so someone made me a target. Not too many people knew where I lived because my parents taught me never to share where I lay my head or how much money I make to the general public. People were always pocket-watching and plotting. So, of those people who did know my address, who could do this? I went down the shortlist of possible suspects in my head before it dawned on me.

Calvin.

I remembered he was supposed to come by to delete the sex tapes we made throughout our sneaky linking, but I don't think I saw his name in my notifications before I cleared them.

"One minute he's harassing me to delete it, and now he's all of a sudden no longer blowing up my phone? Suspicious behavior." I thought to myself. I went back over to my bed, grabbed my phone, and called him.

"Hello?" He answered almost immediately.

I hummed. "I had meant to call you earlier, but I was robbed at gunpoint last night."

"Wait, what?!" He shouted into the phone. "Are you okay?"

"No. I am actually very fucked up about the whole situation. Nobody really knows where I live, and crime isn't a regular occurrence around here, so I'm trying to figure out how I was targeted." I chose my words carefully, making sure to note any changes in his tone.

"Do you still want me to come over?" He asked.

"There's no need for that anymore. The videos and pictures were all deleted." I responded.

He hummed. "Thank you for deleting—"

"I didn't. These robbers did. Super convenient, don't you think?" I quizzed.

"Yeah, that's crazy. I never heard of a robber deleting sex tapes; usually, they'd ask for some type of ransom to keep them from leaking the footage."

"Tell me about it." I chuckled. "Well, seeing as all of our content has been deleted, we no longer have to communicate. Have a great life."

"Yeah."

I hung up the phone and nodded my head in confirmation. He was involved. Collapsing onto the bed, I began to cry. It was clear that I did not know this man at all. How could I have fallen in love with him and didn't know he was capable of being this maniacal? I'd invited him into my home, my life, and the most sacred part of my body.

I can't believe he would put my life in danger. What had I done to make him want to send men to scare me like this? If the sex tapes were such a big deal, he should have handled it like a grown-up instead of a scary-ass bitch.

Calvin knew about my mental health issues. I remember vividly confiding in him one night and for things to turn out like this? I was at a loss for words.

It was a night like any other we'd share. The red LED lights were on, the music in the background and my blunt dangling between my fingers.

Calvin and I had just finished our third round of mind-blowing sex and were lying lazily on the bed, with our legs tangled together.

"Have you ever been sober?" Calvin asked, catching me off guard from my thoughts.

I shrugged. "The weed and alcohol help me deal with everything I have to deal with in my life."

He turned so that we were looking into each other's eyes. "What do you deal with?"

"Depression. I've been battling it for a few years now."

"What caused it? If you don't mind me asking." He had given me his full attention.

I sighed. "My very first relationship was very toxic, in every definition of the word. I thought we were in love, but after I finally let him take my virginity, he broke up with me and told all his homies I was an easy fuck. Men were approaching me, treating me like I was selling pussy for forty dollars. I felt so worthless and used. For months, I dealt with harassment. I fell into a deep depression and almost took my life. I was on the verge of self-harming when Tiana saved me. We had a smoke session with alcohol and some top-of-the-shelf weed that made me feel numb to all the bullshit I'd been dealing with. Ever since that day, I coped with my issues by self-medicating."

Calvin looked like he was on the verge of crying while I shared my story. He pulled me close and rubbed soothing circles on my back. "I'm so sorry you had to experience that, and I'm glad we get to share these moments now."

He sounded so genuine that night, but I see now that he was no different than the men I encountered before him. I was done with him. He'd better hope I never see him again because I didn't know what I would do if we crossed paths.

• •

Finishing the blunt, I looked over at Tiana with a smile. I knew we had similar looks of intoxication. We had hotboxed her car before Derrick's event.

"Let's take a shot before we go in," I pulled a small bottle of Hennessy out of my purse.

"Bitch you built different," Tiana commented. "I'll still take a small sip, though."

After she took a swig of the Hennessy, I drank some of the liquor like it was juice and twisted the top off. We checked our makeup one more time and finally made our appearance at the event. When we walked in, live music and light chatter greeted us. Tables filled with merchandise and artwork stood on display around the venue. Everyone in the area looked as if they were having a lot of fun. I skimmed the room and spotted Derrick. When we locked eyes, he began walking over to us.

"Finally, I almost thought y'all wasn't going to come." Derrick pulled us both into a hug. "Y'all look high as fuck."

"And is," I responded with a light chuckle.

"We're feeling quite astronomical if I do say so myself." Tiana's comment sent us both into a fit of hearty laughter.

"Y'all are a mess," Derrick chuckled. "Anyways, there is food, drinks, and a lot of talented people selling their merchandise. Mingle and enjoy the event."

"We will."

Tiana and I strolled around the event, sampling the food, enjoying the music, and having a great time. That is until we came across Calvin's art setup. My smile morphed into a frown as I eyed the man a few feet in front of me. He had a smile stretching across his face as he showed off his available canvases. I was about to ignore his entire presence when I saw a woman sitting at his table, rubbing her very round belly bump. Something in me snapped.

"I'm about to choose violence, so in case we need to run… be ready for whatever," I warned Tiana as I slowly stepped towards Calvin and his fiancée. I resembled a lioness stalking her prey as I neared the table. Stopping right in front of the woman, I allowed a sinister smile to spread across my face as the horror of the situation dawned on Calvin. He looked like he had seen a ghost the way his usually vibrant skin had turned pale.

"You are so beautiful," I complimented his fiancée. "I would have thought you looked like a gremlin or a whale the way Calvin would spend all those nights in my bed." My voice was so smooth and unwavering that the woman looked at me for a long time, trying to process what I had said.

"Excuse me?" She asked finally, confusion prevalent on her face.

I cleared my throat. "Oh, where are my manners? Hi, I'm Chelsea, and I've been fucking your fiancé for months."

Everyone within hearing distance stopped what they were doing and gasped at my confession. I had a small audience gathering to see this soap opera-like altercation play out.

The pregnant fiancée looked lost for words, and I almost felt bad for bringing stress into her life like this, but I refuse to let her continue to lay with this man without knowing he's been creeping with me.

"I met him at one of these events, and he talked me right out of my panties. I invited him back to my house for a one-night stand, but that night turned into multiple nights until it felt like we saw each other every night. How was he dropping dick off with me while supposedly taking care of you? By the looks of it, you should be giving birth to his child any day now, huh? To have almost cheated on you your entire pregnancy, he couldn't have been the best baby father."

She looked at Calvin with teary eyes. "Is this true?" Her voice was barely above a whisper as she asked this question.

"Hell naw, this ain't true, baby!" Calvin cried out. "This bitch is obviously delusional!"

I chuckled. "I'm delusional, but you got your cousins Ray Ray and Day Day to rob me at gunpoint?!"

"That wasn't me."

"Bullshit. How did the robbers even know about a sex tape? The funny thing is, they sent it to themselves before they deleted the files off my phone, so I still have a copy saved." I smirked at the defeated look on his face. "Would you like to see?" I asked his fiancée.

She aggressively wiped at the tears flowing from her eyes like a waterfall. "Yes."

I pulled out my phone and scrolled a little bit before handing her the device. At total volume, my moans and Calvin's grunts filled the air. I watched as her hand trembled as she looked at the video on the screen. It was undeniable that her fiancé was the male companion in the film.

"Baby, let me—"

"I... I can't breathe," She gasped for air as she began to pant repeatedly. Her chest heaved as she continued to struggle.

"Somebody call 911!" Calvin shouted as his fiancée went limp in the chair she was sitting in.

The smirk that I had morphed into one of panic as I watched in shock as the scene played out.

This was not a part of the plan.

Six

Calvin

Pacing back and forth in the waiting room, I prayed to God that Candace made it through this. I was a complete idiot to think that everything I had done in the dark wouldn't come to light. I had fucked up tremendously and wanted nothing more than for my girls to be okay. I would right all of my wrongs and stay out of trouble for good if God kept them safe.

I underestimated Chelsea. I would never have thought she'd be an angry black woman out to see a black man suffer. I couldn't believe she had actually confronted Candace and me at the event and had proof of the wrong I was doing.

My phone rang, and I scoffed at the name on display. "What do you want?" I seethed into the phone when I answered.

"Where are you? Can I come keep you company and talk to you?" She asked, her voice soft and inviting.

"You must be smoking dick if you think I'm going to sit down and kumbaya with you after the shit you pulled," I growled into the phone.

She smacked her lips. "Calvin, be real with yourself. You are not Mister Perfect, and we have a lot to discuss."

"My wife and child are fighting for their lives," I pointed out.

"And they can do that while we squash this beef."

"What beef?"

"You had men come to my house and rob me at gunpoint. The *least* you could do is have a sit down with me."

"I'll drop a pin, be quick." I hung up without another word and sent her my location. I had to confront my demons in order to move forward with my relationship with Candace. I prayed to the most high that she would be okay and take me back after all of this. I had to be a grown-up about it.

Within twenty minutes, I was sitting in the waiting room with Chelsea beside me. I was sipping on a bottle of water while she sat quietly, fiddling with her thumbs.

"So, are we going to talk or what?" I asked, growing irritated by the second.

She lifted her shoulders, shrugging. "I didn't come here to hold my tongue. I was just gathering my thoughts before I spoke."

"I'm listening."

"Calvin, I promise I did not mean to overwhelm your fiancée like that. I don't know if it was the liquor in my system or the anger of everything that has happened with us the last few weeks, but I swear I didn't want to cause her any harm." Chelsea began her speech.

"Okay, well you did—"

"You're not innocent and free of any responsibility in this situation. You had men rob me at gunpoint! You put my life in jeopardy—"

"I knew they weren't going to hurt you, though. I gave them strict instructions not to harm you in any way." I explained.

"I didn't." Chelsea chuckled. "I was terrified for my life which is saying a lot. You know I confided in you multiple times about my mental health. You said you'd never hurt me or contribute to my bad days. You told me on several occasions that I could trust you to be there if I ever felt suicidal again, yet here we are." She sniffed, wiping at the tears that had slid down her cheeks.

I had honestly forgotten about her depression and struggles with her mental health. I felt like shit as I remembered the nights she'd laid in my arms and told me about her battle. "It was never supposed to get to this point. I should have ended things months ago," I sighed.

"Should've. Would've. Could've." She shook her head. "You approached me knowing good and well that you were in a relationship with a woman who was having your baby. You continued to play the game, sneaky linking with me when you should have been home with your fiancée and son. You are in the wrong. All of the shit that happened as a result of your dirty dick deeds! You need to take full responsibility for the shit that you caused. I am not the bad guy here. I may have reacted a bit overboard, but that's nothing compared to what I could have done!" She was yelling now. "You could have left me alone! You could have never spoken to me, to begin with, yet you smooth-talked me out of my draws and continued to fuck me until I was in too deep. I fell in love with your essence. I fell in love with the way our bodies fit so perfectly together. I fell in love with the idea that when we were together, it was like a fairytale. I was addicted to your scent, your taste, your touch, and especially your dick. Yet, you didn't view me in the same light. I was nothing more than a pastime." She had a steady stream of tears falling from her eyes.

I resembled a fish out of the water as I opened and closed my mouth a few times, figuring out how to respond. I felt like complete shit. "I'm sorry."

"No, you're not. You're only sorry that you weren't able to keep your lies in order." She responded, wiping at her tear-stained cheeks.

"Both." I sighed, wrapping an arm around her shoulder. "I was selfish. When I was with you, you unlocked a creative side that I didn't even know I had. I used you as my muse. The energy you possess is so inviting that I didn't want you to allow anyone else in. I didn't want anyone else to use you the way I was." I explained honestly. Chelsea's energy was unlike any other woman I'd ever met. She had a way of organically attracting me to her very core. The sex was intoxicating because our energies were as if they were on the same wavelength.

"Well, you hurt me in the process of being selfish. If it weren't for the drugs and liquor I consume daily, I may have relapsed and tried to take my life again. You made me feel so dirty and used, despite all the times you promised you wouldn't treat me like the other men in my past. Yet here we are."

"I know, and I apologize."

"Okay."

"So do we stop all communication for good now?"

"I do want to make sure your fiancée is okay and apologize to her for causing this hospital visit." She added.

I nodded. "I'm sure Candy doesn't want to see the both of us walking into her hospital room, but I'll give her the heads up and set up a time when you can meet up with her. Right now, though, I don't think that's a good idea."

"You're right."

We stood up. "There's a lot of women who wouldn't sit down and have a conversation with a man who did them dirty. It truly shows your growth and character that you were able to sit down with me and discuss this without getting physical."

"Trust me; I wanted to put my hands on you. I wanted to beat your ass and make you pay for breaking my heart. I thought you were different, but I realized that I attract these types of men and need to reevaluate myself before I share my body and time with anyone else."

"Good luck with that."

"Mhm," She grabbed her stuff. "I guess I'll let you be."

"Again, I'm so sorry for how everything played out."

"Mhm."

I swiped my thumb against her soft face and then leaned down to press a soft peck onto her cheek. "I wish you the best."

"I wanted you to suffer, but I am a firm believer in Karma, so you will get what you deserve in life." She left without another word.

Shortly after Chelsea's departure, the doctor walked into the waiting area and told me that I could go to Candace's room. I had never jumped up from my seat so fast in my life. I grabbed my belongings and practically sprinted into the room where my fiancée sat in bed, holding our precious baby girl in her arms.

I walked over to the bed and stared at the small child for a long moment. "She's so beautiful."

"She's perfect." Candace agreed.

"Can I hold her?"

"Yeah."

I scooped the newborn baby into my arms and sat in the cushioned chair beside the bed. I looked at the soft, innocent face of my daughter, and a wave of emotions engulfed me. "Daddy loves you, baby girl," I said in a voice barely above a whisper.

She blinked her eyes until they adjusted to the light and stared at me. At that moment, I knew that I had to change my ways. "I'm going to be an example of the kind of man you should want in your life. I am going to spoil you and treat you like the princess you were born to be. You won't have to worry about a thing. I put that on everything I love; I'm a changed man."

"Don't sit there and lie to our child." Candace rolled her eyes.

"I'm serious."

"If you ain't change for CJ, why should I believe that you're going to change for Cierra? Let's be real for a second. The only reason you proposed to me was because I got pregnant. You never had any plans to get serious with me. You were just being selfish and didn't want me going out and having fun like you continued to do throughout our relationship."

I was once again at a loss for words. She'd never talked to me like this, and it honestly caught me off guard. "What are you talking about?" I asked, confused.

"Don't play dumb now. You were never sneaky when it came to your cheating. I knew about all of the women you slept with behind my back. From the beginning of our relationship to now, I wanted you to confess. I wanted you to tell me why I was never enough for you, but I always just held my tongue." She wiped at her tears. "I gave you two kids! I put my career on hold to be the perfect girlfriend and mother, just for you to come and go and expose me to who knows what kind of diseases and demons."

"Baby—"

"No! You are going to sit there and listen to me!" She raised her voice, causing our daughter to let out a soft whimper. I gently rocked her in my arms until she closed her eyes and let out a sigh of content.

"Yes ma'am."

"Years. I gave you *years* of my life for you to mistreat me. You continuously cheated, and the worst part of all is you thought I would be complacent and blind to the late nights, constant calls, and sex tapes. Do I really look that stupid to you?"

"No, it was never like that."

"What is it then? Is my pussy trash? My personality? What caused you to constantly cheat on me while I was at home with your son and unborn child growing inside of me?! What was the reason for you to risk not only your life but my life as well in these streets fucking on all these different women?"

Once again, I resembled a fish out of the water as I struggled to collect my thoughts. Once again, I was against the ropes because I had underestimated my opponent. I should have known Candace wasn't a fool. I should have known that all of my cheating and lies would catch up to me in the end.

"I…"

"Do you need more time to get your lies in order? Why can't you just be straight up with me, Calvin? Do you even want to get married?"

"Baby, yes, I want to spend the rest of my life with you—"

I was cut off again. "With all your extra side pieces, huh?"

"No." I let out a frustrated sigh and stood up. I walked over to the corner of the room, placing our baby in the crib the nurse rolled in. I made sure she was secure and safe before I walked over to Candace, sat on the edge of the bed, and held her hand.

"Here comes the Oscar-winning performance." Candace rolled her eyes.

"No theatrics, no performance. I'm finna speak from my heart, and hopefully, when I finish, you decide to continue to be my woman." I took a deep breath and began pouring my heart and soul out to her. "I didn't have some bad childhood or traumatic experience to make me a better man. My life was always boring, but I could bring some creativity to my life through my art. I created my best work when I share a night with a new woman. This isn't my excuse, but I got my inspiration from pillow talking with women and hearing their stories."

"So, you're a serial cheater because of the inspiration you get from sticking your dick in other women? Why not just be single?" She questioned.

"I never thought I'd get in a serious relationship this early in my life. I planned to be single through my entire twenties to explore and live my best life. I was sticking to that until I met you. You captivated me with your beauty and personality. You drew me in and made me want to do things I'd never done with a woman before. You made me want to go on dates and all that other romantic shit. I was used to the late nights full of sex and then going on about my day, but with you…" I drifted off into a deep reflection.

"You tapped into a part of me that wanted to wake up the next morning with you laying on my chest in bed." I caressed the back of her hand as I remember the early days of our relationship.

"So, what changed?"

I shrugged. "The old me and the new me were at odds with what to do. I wanted to be faithful to you, but that little voice kept telling me to go out and keep exploring, keep indulging in the sex with random women. I wasn't going to do it forever, but I did get caught up in the feeling when I met Chelsea. I had convinced myself that if I stopped fucking all those random women and just kept one on the side, I made progress into being a better man. I had ended things with Chelsea when everything kind of blew up in my face."

"So here we are."

"You are the woman I want to spend the rest of my life with."

"You don't even know me. If you did know me, you would've known that instead of cheating on me, we could have been fucking these women together, but no. You wanted to do things sneakily and ruin our relationship." Candace responded.

"Wait, huh?"

"Yeah, I've always been into threesomes and shit, but you are just so selfish." She shrugged.

The thought of a night with Candace and Chelsea crossed my mind, and I immediately adjusted myself. "Too late for that now?"

"When I'm all healed, we can test those waters."

"So, I didn't lose my wife?"

"No, but this is your last chance to make it right. There will be no more stepping out. When we say those vows, you are mine and mine only. We can bring someone into the bedroom, but only if we both agree. Just stop embarrassing me out here in these streets."

"I got you!"

I pressed my lips against hers softly. This conversation with Candace definitely did not go as I had expected.

Seven

Chelsea

Six months later

"Are you sure you want to do this?" Tiana asked through the phone.

I nodded. "I'm curious to see how this will go. I've never been invited to a threesome before. Also, to do it with someone as fine as Calvin and his wife? What could possibly go wrong?"

"Am I the only one who remembers you exposing your affair with her husband? Am I the only one who remembers you being the side chick? Am I the only one who remembers you shocking that woman into labor?! There's a lot that could go wrong with you having sex with them tonight."

"It might not even lead to sex. We're going out on a date, and if things progress organically into something more, then so be it. I'm entering with an open mind, and they're entering with a clean slate. Everything should be fine!" I explained the best I could, but I knew that Tiana wouldn't understand. This was a complicated situation, and even the most open-minded person wouldn't usually agree to go out with a man and his wife.

A part of me was always curious about threesomes and polygamy. I just never thought the opportunity would arise, especially from a situation where so much drama occurred.

"It's almost 7. I'm going to talk to you either tonight or tomorrow, depending on how things go." I put on the final touches of my outfit as I gathered my thoughts and ended the call. I did a once-over in the mirror, making sure my lingerie wasn't visible before leaving my home and getting into my car.

The entire drive had my stomach in knots, indicating that I was nervous. The nerves didn't subside even after I took two blunts to the head. I was high as hell, which made me even more self-conscious about tonight. All I wanted was for this night to go smoothly. I wanted to make a great impression with Candace and have mind-boggling sex with both of them all night. I wanted to experience a level of ecstasy that I'd never even dreamed of. I just wasn't sure she'd be receptive to me. I had caused her a lot of pain and suffering. I made her go into early labor. Of course, I apologized a dozen times, but that doubt and skepticism made me nervous about this meet-up.

I'd been wronged so many times before; I had a tiny sliver of doubt that tonight would go horribly wrong, and I end my life. I just hope that those terrible thoughts would all go away when I finally sit down and enjoy the night with them.

As I pulled into the front of the hotel, my mouth damn near dropped to the ground. I got out of the car and handed my keys to the valet. Afterward, I made my way through the hotel to the elevator. I pressed the top floor and waited patiently as the elevator rose. When the elevator stopped, I felt nauseous as I walked down the long carpeted hallway to the suite at the very end. I knocked three times and waited for a few moments before the door swung open.

"Hello beautiful," Candace greeted me with a smile so bright, it washed away all of the nerves I had about tonight. That one inviting smile reassured me that tonight would be great.

I returned her smile with a shy smile of my own and stepped into the hotel room. The room was beautiful. The hotel room was decorated with candles, rose petals, and soft r&b music. The lights were dimly lit, and from my view near the bed, I could see a candlelit dinner on the balcony waiting for us.

"Wow." I let out a breath as I took in the whole scene around me. "This is all so beautiful. I've never had anyone do something so… romantic for me before." I confessed. This was all foreign. I knew that if I thought about it too long, I'd shed tears.

"You deserve to be romanced. We plan to romance you all night long." Calvin emerged from the bathroom and held out a rose for me. "You look beautiful."

"Thank you." I could feel my face heat up. "Y'all got me feeling like a schoolgirl. I can't believe I'm acting like this."

"We're about to make you feel things you've never felt all night. Tonight will definitely be a night to remember, baby." Candace grabbed my hand and led me outside. We all sat around the table and began eating the meal.

"I'm not even going to lie to y'all," I began. "I was so nervous about tonight."

"We were too." Candace chuckled. "I was so nervous that you wouldn't like me and that I would have to beat your ass."

"Beat my ass?"

"If we got to the sexy fun and you only focus on my man. I'd beat yo ass all the way to Canada and back."

I laughed. "I was nervous that this was all a setup, and when I knocked on the door, you would beat my ass."

"Not y'all both resulted to violence in these hypothetical worlds." Calvin chuckled.

"Well, we didn't meet on the best of terms, but here we are. I have an open mind about the situation, but I wasn't sure y'all would."

Candace took a sip of her wine. "Let me just say that I would have been all for threesomes before y'all's little love affair. I told Calvin the night Cierra was born that if he'd have gone about this the right way, we would have avoided all drama and been doing threesomes together."

"Now, we're going to see how it works," Calvin added. "I get to have you and my beautiful wife together tonight. Best of both worlds."

I could feel my excitement building in my core. I was growing hotter every time they mentioned the plans we'd put into action tonight.

"How do y'all want tonight to go? I'm not very informed about how things are supposed to go," I spoke to them honestly. "Is everybody touching everybody? Is anything off-limits?"

"Have you ever been with a woman before?"

"Once."

I had experimented in college a bit. I had always thought women were beautiful and indulged in lesbian porn every now and then, but I had never really considered myself bisexual until recently.

"I think we should just see how things progress naturally. I'm going to make sure both of you are cumming all night; how you reach those nuts will be up for exploration."

I shifted in my seat. "So what are we waiting for?"

"Skip the small talk and go straight to the bed?" Candace smirked.

I bit down on my bottom lip. "I've been waiting to see if your lips are as soft as they look, so yes, please."

Within a few moments, we were in the hotel room, removing our clothes. Calvin was lying on the bed with his back pressed against the headboard as he stroked his member. He had his eyes trained on me and Candace, who were both naked, exploring each other's bodies.

Candace's lips were so soft against my skin that the mere brush of skin to skin sent chills down my spine. I tilted my head to expose my neck and allowed her to slide her tongue along the length of my neck before she settled on the area she was most fond of and sunk her teeth firmly against the skin. I let out a soft moan as I rubbed my hands along the curves and dips of her body as she tasted different parts of me.

"You like this baby?" Candace purred in my ear so seductively that I visibly shook with anticipation.

"Yes." I breathed, biting down on my lips as she trailed her fingers between my thighs.

"Damn, you're so wet." She commented, sliding her middle and pointer finger along the crease of my lips.

"C'mere," Calvin's voice was drenched with lust as he spoke to me. I moved from the edge of the bed to the middle, where he sat stroking his dick firmly. I was on all fours in front of his fully erect member as I replaced his hands with my mouth.

"Fuck." The throaty groan that followed indicated that Calvin definitely enjoyed the switch.

I was doing the double hand twist and suck when I felt a slap on my ass. I let out a moan around his throbbing member while Candace slid behind me and spread my cheeks. She stuck a thumb in my ass and began eating my pussy so good; my legs began to shake. I wasn't a bitch, but I was struggling to keep sucking his dick.

"Fuck!" I had tears flowing from my eyes due to the pleasure of Candace's actions and the fact that I was choking on Calvin's dick.

We spent nearly an hour on foreplay and oral sex. I'd nutted three times and couldn't believe we were still going at it like professional pornstars. When we had finally started experimenting with different sexual positions, I was completely fulfilled. I was riding Calvin's dick, rocking my hips like I was hula-hooping while Candace rode his face; she was practically twerking on his tongue. I had one of her titties in my hand while we tongue kissed on top of Calvin.

If I was out of shape, I'm sure all of the physical activity would've sent me into an asthma attack. We were doing things I'd never even seen in the porn films, and I'd watched plenty of clips in my day.

"You like this dick?" Calvin asked Candace as he twisted her like a pretzel and pounded into her.

"I love this dick, daddy." Candace moaned as she looked over at me and licked her lips. "Let me play with that pussy, baby."

I had been sitting this round out, smoking my blunt and watching, when Candace called me over. I slid over so that I was within reach of her and let her rub my lips. She inserted two fingers inside of me and made the come here motion with her middle and ring finger. I continued to smoke my blunt while she fingered me. Calvin continued to pound into Candace, and it was honestly a beautiful sight to see.

All night, we switched positions, climaxed, and did it again. It was like we were playing a game of twister without the mat. When we finally called it quits, the sun had begun to peek from behind the curtains of the hotel room windows. I was lying in bed, staring at the ceiling while Candace and Calvin laid on either side of me, sleeping peacefully.

The time I spent with the two of them was something I didn't want to end. I knew that I was probably never going to experience this feeling again. This was probably going to be a one-time thing, and I'd have to go back to using my toys until I find another suitable partner.

"Everything okay, baby?" Candace asked as she snuggled up to me and caressed my cheek.

"Just thinking about how this was such an amazing night that I probably won't ever experience again," I spoke honestly.

She rubbed my body gently. "Who said this had to end?"

My eyebrows rose with curiosity. "Y'all want to keep doing this?"

"Absolutely." She smiled so bright that I felt goosebumps rise onto my skin. "I enjoyed this. I know Calvin enjoyed this. So, knowing that everybody was satisfied, we should keep doing it."

"I'd love that."

"Me too."

I allowed her to move until she was lying on top of me. With our legs tangled in the sheets, she pressed her lips against mine. I immediately slid my tongue along her bottom lip, and she granted me access. One thing I will never forget at this moment was how Candace made me a water fountain when she touched my body. When I slid my hand between us and rubbed her pussy slowly, she moaned against my mouth.

"Do you want to take it to the bathroom?"

"We can."

We silently got out of the bed, making sure not to disturb Calvin, and went into the bathroom and turned on the shower. We stepped into the shower and immediately began to explore each other's bodies. I pressed her up against the shower wall and hiked one of her legs up. I detached the showerhead and aimed it against her clit. She squirmed and moaned out in pleasure.

"You like that?"

"Yes." She pulled me close and stuck her tongue in my mouth.

"I want you to cum for me, baby," I instructed, using my other hand to insert two fingers inside of her while keeping the shower head aimed at her clit. She damn near convulsed like she was getting exorcised when she came onto my fingers. I removed my hand and stuck my fingers in her mouth. "How do you taste?"

"You tell me." She stuck her tongue in my mouth again, swirling it all over. "My turn." She pushed me up against the shower wall and leaned in.

"I'm going to make you cum so hard; you're going to forget how your legs work." She spoke just slightly above a whisper against my ear. She was ignoring my throbbing pussy, so I reached my hand down to rub my neglected clit.

"Did I tell you to touch yourself?" She growled in my ear.

"No," I responded breathlessly.

She smirked and swatted my hand away. "Don't touch this pussy without my permission."

That phrase sent a spark straight to my pussy, making the wet area throb with excitement. I wanted her to touch me so badly, I almost begged for it.

"Close your eyes." She instructed. I did. "I want you to spread your legs." I did. "I want you to put your hands above your head and don't move them." I did.

"Touch me, please." I whimpered like a mouse trapped by a cat.

"Shh," She licked my neck like a lion tasting their prey. I moved my arms to caress her soft, wet skin, but she moved away. "Did I say you could touch me?"

"No," I whined.

She turned me around and gave my ass a firm smack. "Listen to me, baby."

"I just want you to fuck me up against this wall."

She smirked. "I can do that."

She knew exactly how to please me. She sucked on my titties while she pumped her fingers inside of me. She did it tantalizingly slow, which brought tears to my eyes. She hit my g-spot with every pump, causing my body to shiver.

"I'm about to c—"

"Hold that shit in, baby." She sped up the pumps of her fingers.

"I can't hold it much longer."

"Yes, you can."

"I—" My body jolted forward as I squirted all over the shower floor. I slumped against her body, and she patted my pussy, as if saying, 'Good job.'

"You did good, baby."

"Mmm," I moaned, unable to coherently put words together to form sentences.

"I know you're tired. Let's lay down?" She asked.

I nodded and allowed her to guide me to the bedroom, where we rejoined Calvin, who was still sleeping.

I could get used to this.

Eight

Calvin

"Good morning, baby," Candace purred into my ear as she kissed and nibbled on my earlobe.

"Good morning, beautiful."

I wrapped my arms around her waist and pulled her on top of me; straddling my hips, she cocked her head to the side to look at me with her lust-filled eyes. After she licked my neck teasingly slow, she slid her naked lower region up and down my length at the pace of a snail.

"You are playing," I commented while slapping her ass firmly.

"So what if I am?" She questioned.

"You want to find out?"

She hummed, biting down on her lip and trailing her pointer finger down the length of my chest to my belly button. She circled my belly button and made her way underneath the covers until she was eye to tip with my hard dick. She licked the length of my dick before wrapping her lips around the head and sucking on it like a tootsie roll lollipop. I put my arms behind my head and looked up at the ceiling. A smile stretched across my face as I felt like the luckiest man in the world.

I was living every man's dream. I had my wife, two kids, and a woman who enjoyed threesomes with us. It had felt like everything had fallen into place. I wish I had been upfront about my needs in the beginning so that I could have been experiencing this longer.

I was sitting here thinking about all of the dirt I had done behind Candace's back just to end up in a situation where we're both honest about our discretions. We didn't do anything without the other knowing, and it honestly felt good not to have to lie to her anymore.

"I'm about to—" Candace sucked me like a vacuum, making me moan lowly while my toes began to curl. I tensed up, and my hips jerked upward as I shot my load into her mouth. She didn't stop sucking until she'd milked all of the thick, white substance into her mouth and licked any excess from my length. We stood up from the bed and went into the bathroom to get our day started. We showered together, and as we stood in the bathroom brushing our teeth beside each other, I looked at her with a bright smile.

"I love you," I spoke after spitting my toothpaste into the sink. I poured mouth wash into my mouth and began gargling.

"How would you feel about making Chelsea our girlfriend?"

I choked on the minty liquid in my mouth, which caused me to hunch over and spit out the fluid into the sink. "Huh?"

"I really like her. I don't want her to go out and share that pussy with nobody else. I want her to be our girlfriend, so she feels comfortable not fucking with anybody else. We'll take care of her." Candace explained.

I was honestly surprised to hear those words come out of her mouth. It was like I was talking to a stranger. Candace had never acted like this before, and since bringing Chelsea into our bedroom, I could see her changing before my eyes.

"You sure she'd be up for this?"

"Although you haven't gotten to know her outside of the sex, we talk and spend time together all the time when we're not working. She's great with the kids but doesn't want any of her own. Because of her opinions of kids, this would be a bonus for her. She gets to experience a family without the commitment of having a pregnancy herself. She absolutely *loves* the intimate moments we share, and I know this is exactly what she needs to help battle her depression. She needs something concrete and real." Candace began this long tangent about Chelsea, and I was shocked. I never considered any of this when I was fucking Chelsea because I didn't care. I realized that I was no different than the men she'd tell me about between our sessions of sex. I only cared about the sex and the art I created when I was around her. I was selfish as hell, which made me feel like shit.

Since this whole arrangement began, Candace was building a real relationship with Chelsea. Our different approaches showed how different male and female reactions to sex are. She wanted to connect with Chelsea on the highest of levels. Throughout the duration I had spent with Chelsea alone, I only focused on the surface-level aspects to distance myself from catching any type of feelings.

"You put a lot of thought into this, huh?"

She affirmed with a nod. "I have. I've really grown a soft spot for her. She's been through so much, and I really want to make her feel loved and appreciated. I don't want her to subject herself to a life of temporary pleasure. She deserves long-term happiness."

"So, what's the plan?" I asked. "I'm not opposed to the idea. I know a lot of people in polygamous relationships that have found it to be cool. I'm just not sure it would last very long."

"Why?"

"We're married. I assume one day Chelsea would want a ring of her own."

"Okay? Our loyalty and understanding exceed anything else. A ring would be a bonus to the love and security we'd be giving her." Candace had already come to her conclusion of how things would play out, and I knew that any objection I had would be met with a calculated response.

"This is what you really want?"

"Yes."

"Okay. We can take her out on a nice date and ask her to be our girlfriend. I have to get a few hours in with some potential clients, but find a babysitter and keep me in the loop with the plans."

"Yessir!" A grin stretched across her beautiful face, and I returned one of my own. "This is going to be the start of something spectacular!"

"Your happiness is all that I am concerned about at the end of the day. Whatever you need, just call me. I have to get going."

"I love you!"

"I love you more!"

As we finished our morning routines in the bathroom, Candace tied a robe around her body. Disappearing out of the bathroom, she most likely went to tend to the kids. I got dressed in comfortable clothing and headed out of the house.

• •

"Wow," Chelsea took in the scenery around her with bright, inviting eyes. "I've never been treated like this before."

"We hope to be your first for a lot of things. You deserve to live a life full of excitement and adventure." Candace spoke up. I showed my agreement with a slight nod of my head.

"Y'all didn't have to do all of this for me." Chelsea wiped at her teary eyes as she sat down on the blanket laid out on the sand. She grabbed a cup of the chilled wine and took a sip. "This is all too much."

Candace had called a babysitter, her mom, to come and watch the kids while we took Chelsea out to our beach house and set up a romantic beach dinner. It consisted of a meat lasagna, salad, and garlic bread. Candace set up the candles and picked out the wine for the night. She also made sure to have the speaker playing all of Chelsea's favorite R&B songs. If I weren't secure in our relationship, I'd be jealous of the effort Candace was putting in to make Chelsea feel special. However, I knew that this was a woman thing. Candace and Chelsea were able to connect on a level that I would never relate to with them. As women, their intimacy bond would hold a different level of tenderness and security that I, as a man, would never be able to provide for them.

"You better get used to the treatment. Between Candy and me, we're going to make sure you feel wanted and appreciated every day."

"Thank y'all for this," Chelsea reached out and held our hands.

The dinner went smoothly, and once we finished our meals, we stood up and walked along the beach together. We were all holding hands and just enjoying the aura around us.

"Chels, we were wondering..." I began.

"If you would like to be our girlfriend," Candace finished. We waited for her response as she looked at us with confusion etched across her face.

"Girlfriend?"

"The third addition to our relationship. You'd get the best of both worlds. A family. We'd treat you like the queen you deserve to be treated as." I explained.

Candace pulled Chelsea into a warm embrace, caressing her cheek softly. "Baby, we've gotten to know each other on such a deep and spiritual level that I wouldn't want you to be pampered and pleased by anybody else except us. You'd be the perfect addition to our family."

"Family?"

"Yes, baby."

I watched as they shared this moment. The emotions skirted across Chelsea's features like a slideshow on a projector. She was at a loss for words as she looked between my wife and me.

"I don't know what to say." Chelsea finally spoke.

"A simple, 'I'd love to be your girlfriend' would work." I joked.

Chelsea's smile ignited the evening sky. "I would absolutely love to be y'all's girlfriend."

"Now, I been thinking about fucking the two of you on the beach all night. Please tell me this is the part where we fuck on that blanket and try not to get sand in places sand should not be."

"Most definitely."

We made our way back to the blankets we had set out, and within seconds we discarded our clothes, and our night of ecstasy commenced. The night was magical, to say the least. We did positions I didn't even know were possible. We'd all reached a plethora of climaxes that I was sure we'd have died of dehydration had we not taken water breaks between each round. The intensity of each round of sex made all of my previous sexual encounters seem like amateur hours.

The sounds of our lovemaking would have caused a disturbance had we not been in such a secluded area. The moans and groans combined with the slaps and claps created a harmonious melody into the night's air that I'd never forget. I'd never wanted anything more in life than to spend the rest of my days with these two women I laid with tonight.

After several rounds of electrifying sex, we gathered our belongings and went inside the beach house. We made our way into the shower, where the three of us shared an intimate moment. There was no sex, just the three of us washing and caressing each others' bodies. Once we were all clean and made sure there was no sand in hidden creases, we laid naked in bed, cuddled together and enjoying the sound of nature around us.

"I just want to say that I never thought that I would have an experience like this." Chelsea broke the silence. "I've felt so complete these past couple of months spending these nights with y'all.

I am truly grateful that the two of you decided to bring me into your relationship as a girlfriend. I get the best dick and the best coochie I've ever had in my life." She giggled. "The two of you together make me feel like a virgin again."

"You're so cute, baby." Candace smiled and rubbed her hand along the length of Chelsea's back.

"I'm the luckiest man in the world." Gripping a handful of both of their asses, I grinned happily. "I wouldn't trade this shit in for anything in the world."

"You're our king, and we're going to treat you as such." Candace pulled me into a deep, passionate kiss while I felt Chelsea's hands rubbing my chest softly.

Just at that moment, a spark moved through my body. The urge to paint overcame me. "I need to create," I spoke up.

"Set up the camera. Record our next few rounds. I don't want to stop touching you just yet." Candace proposed.

I nodded. I got out of bed, and the two women moved in closer to each other, immediately locking their lips together and exploring each others' bodies in the process.

I rummaged through my bag until I found the camera and tripod and set the camera up directly in front of the bed. I turned on the lamp to provide dim lighting and returned to the bed to join my beautiful wife and girlfriend.

This next exhibit would be my best work yet. The motivation and inspiration these two were giving me would result in astonishing content. I was optimistic about that.

Who would have thought that my story would end with a wife and a girlfriend and fantastic sex? My life was perfect. Nothing could possibly go wrong.

Nine

Chelsea

I wrapped her hair around my hand like a rope and pulled it firmly. Her back arched, and she let out a moan so sexy, my pussy throbbed with excitement. Everything Candy did turned me on to a degree I never knew I could obtain. If I wasn't sure about my sexuality before, I knew that I was highly attracted to this woman.

"You're so fucking sexy, mamas."

"Thank you, beautiful." She smirked as she threw her ass back onto the strap. She was throwing her ass so powerfully that I had to plant my feet onto the floor firmly to keep from losing my balance. She was a demon in the bedroom but an angel in public. I loved that about her. No one knew how nasty she could get when we were together.

Since meeting Candace, we'd bonded in a way I never thought I would with someone else. It was as if she were my gift from God the way we'd clicked immediately. Our bodies were made for each other. We knew exactly how to please each other. In addition, we learned how to stimulate each other on an intellectual level. Nothing was simply surface-level with us. Everything was more profound, more intense. Physically, mentally, intellectually, and spiritually, Candace was my person.

I thought I was addicted to the way I felt with Calvin, but the moment I got a taste of Candace, she became my true addiction.

I wanted to make her happy, to make her smile, to make her cum repeatedly.

Unlike Calvin, Candace had initiated dates. She wanted to spend time with me outside of the bedroom. It was like she wanted to know the real me. Since meeting her, I cut back on my alcohol and weed consumption. I wasn't completely sober, but I didn't rely on the substances to distract me from my depression. In fact, I didn't have nearly as many depressive episodes since meeting Candace. She was my person. She brought out a glow in me that I didn't even know I had in myself.

"This pussy gets so wet for me," Candace purred in my ear as she rubbed my clit with her thumb. She was pumping her pointer and middle finger inside of me at a steady pace. She sucked and nibbled on my neck in the process.

"You turn me into a water fountain. From the way you kiss me, touch me, lick me, and fuck me. You make my pipes burst every time." I rocked my hips to the pace of the pumps of her fingers, tilting my head slightly so that she'd get the hint and kiss me. We tongue kissed as I rode out my orgasm. I was completely spent after that. I laid on the bed and stared at the spinning ceiling fan.

"Aht aht," Candace grabbed my hand and pulled me into a sitting position. "We need to shower and get ready. We have nail appointments before Calvin's event. This is going to be a big night for us moving forward in our relationship."

"Can I take a nap?" I pushed my lips into a pout and looked up at Candace with begging eyes. I was so tired that my eyelids felt like bricks. I could barely keep them open. I wanted nothing more than to wrap my body around Candy's and sleep until the event.

"The shower will wake you up." She pulled me out of bed and practically dragged me to the shower. She washed my body while I fought the drowsiness that crept into my body.

The shower took about twenty minutes, and then we put on casual clothes to head to the nail salon. We spent a few hours getting complimentary nail sets and then went shopping for our dresses for the evening. The showcase was going to be epic.

Candace and I got lunch and went back to prepare for the event.

• •

"Tonight would not have been possible without these two beautiful women," Calvin raised his glass to initiate a toast on our behave.

I was shy in large public settings, especially when the attention was on me and I couldn't joke my way out of it.

Everyone in the venue raised their glasses as the showcase began. Eight canvases were waiting for their turn to be uncovered. Calvin stood next to the first easel and pulled the covering away to reveal a realistic depiction of the three of us tangled in the bed together. I was truly mesmerized by the artwork on display. I could not remove my eyes from scanning every inch of the canvas in awe.

"This is beautiful." I breathed. Calvin was definitely a talented artist.

"These two women have unlocked a creative side within me that I didn't even know I possessed my damn self. I am so grateful to have them both in my life." Calvin spoke with so much conviction and honesty that I was overcome with so many emotions. I'd never heard him speak so highly of me. I didn't even know he actually cared about me outside of the bedroom. To see that I inspired such beautiful pieces of artwork filled me with an abundance of joy.

"Relax, baby," Candace gave my hand a gentle squeeze, instantly easing the tension that was building throughout my body. "Good job, baby."

The night was filled with talented artwork, great music, and delicious champagne.

When the evening was over, we went back to their place, and I cooked them a meal. I made Cajun chicken pasta with garlic knots and a side of salad. We sat at the table, ate in comfortable silence, and opened up a bottle of delicious semi-sweet red wine.

"These past few months with y'all have been so amazing. I've never felt so loved and appreciated before in my life. I want to thank both of you, especially Candace, for taking the time to get to know the real me, flaws and all. I've cut back on my alcohol and weed consumption because the way you two make me feel is better than any temporary feeling I'd get from drinking until I'm drunk or smoking until I'm numb." I poured my heart and soul out to the two people sitting around the table.

"Not you are getting all emotional," Candace teased, smiling brightly at me.

I chuckled, wiping at my teary eyes. "Shut up!"

"The two of you made me a better man," Calvin spoke up. "Y'all unlocked a part of me that I didn't even know existed. I want to thank y'all."

"Not both of y'all getting all mushy gushy on me." Candace was full of jokes tonight. She was indeed a gift from God. If I was Calvin, I damn sure wouldn't have wanted to share this woman with anybody else. I would have given her the world on a silver platter without a second thought. Hell, I wanted to give her everything she deserved and more, and we'd only been fooling around for a few months.

I'd confront a lot of my demons in the last few months in hopes of bettering myself to be the best girlfriend I could be for them. I was not about to mess up this opportunity. This was what I'd needed all along.

This was the life I deserved. I would hold on to this moment for as long as I could. I never wanted this fairytale to end.

Ten

Omniscient

Two years later

"Are you ready?" Tiana questioned as she made final touches to Chelsea's hair. The long extensions falling into loose curls down her back.

Today was the day Chelsea and Candace would be tying the knot and taking their relationship to the next level. This had been a long, eventful two years for the couple. For one, Candace had gone through a nasty divorce a year back when her husband stepped out once again and brought a sexually transmitted disease into their home.

The trio had been going strong for almost five months when Calvin grew tired of the two women who had grown very close as time progressed. Calvin felt like an outsider in his relationship and began spending more time outside of the home, going to events, and working late in his studio.

History was known to repeat itself, and Calvin met a young woman at an event and went back to her place; unluckily for him, this woman had given him gonorrhea. For a while, they ignored the symptoms until everything became unbearable. When they went to the clinic and found out what was causing their discomfort, a huge fight broke out.

"Gonorrhea?! Where the fuck did you contract gonorrhea?!" Candace was furious as she threw the test results at Calvin.

"How do you know it was me who brought it into our home?! Do you know where Chelsea is at all times?" Calvin argued back.

Chelsea had been quiet up until this point. She stood up and looked at Calvin with pure hatred in her eyes. "First of all, I'm at this house more than you are. I spend the majority of my time here with Candy and your kids. Unlike your cheating ass, I take care of them. I'm putting in more effort than you are. Second of all, even when we first met, I was an advocate for regular testing. That hasn't changed and never will. I took pride in myself for being sexually healthy. You're the dirty dick nigga with the terrible track record for stepping out on his family. You're the dirty dick nigga with a history of cheating. Why would you cheat on two women who milk your dick until there's no nut left to bust? Yet here we are. I love Candy too much to ever want to ruin our relationship by even putting myself in a situation that could open our home to sexually transmitted infections."

"If you have a fear of commitment, just say that." Candace wiped at her tear-stricken cheeks. "You know what, I want a divorce. You treated me like a toss-a-way for too long. I forgave you time and time again, and this is how you treat me? The mother of your children? Fuck you, disrespectfully."

Calvin's face resembled one of sheer horror. He looked between the two women in front of him and knew his infidelities had finally caught up to him. "I'm sorry."

"No, you're not. You are never sorry. You're literally a serial cheater. You don't know how to be loyal. You're going to put yourself in a lot of unnecessary drama because you can't keep your fucking dick to yourself." Candace wiped at her eyes angrily. "Do you see how much you've hurt me over the years? Like a dummy, I opened our relationship to a woman I knew you were fond of, and that still wasn't enough for you. I'm done trying because this just goes to show that you don't care about me. You never have."

"So, we're done?"

"Finished. Completely. No more tries. No more forgiveness. You made your bed now lie in it."

Candace meant every word she spoke that day because that very same week, she had her lawyers write up the divorce papers. She wanted this to go as smoothly as possible for the sake of her children. She was a mother of two, and they were flourishing in everything they did. Calvin Junior expressed his creative side through dancing and music. Cierra conveyed herself through fashion. Candace made sure that they had the freedom to express themselves as much as they wanted no matter what.

The divorce ended with the Candace and Calvin agreeing that they would have joint custody, but Calvin would only get certain weekends with his kids. He didn't object to that because he spent most of his time in the studio anyway, which would limit this time he'd have with his kids.

The divorce did the two of them well. Calvin was able to come to terms with the fact that he was not meant to settle down and live a monogamous lifestyle; hell, the idea of settling down in a polygamous relationship didn't appeal to him either. Realizing that it was him and not the women he slept with, Calvin apologized to both Candace and Chelsea for everything he put them through.

For a long time, the two women kept things platonic until they realized that their love for each other went far more profound than friendship and occasional sex. They discovered that the universe put them in this world together, and they were soulmates. This realization was what ultimately led Candace to propose to Chelsea.

It was an ordinary sunny afternoon when Candace took the kids to the park with Chelsea. Candace had sat on the bench a few feet away and watched as they all enjoyed their time together, running to the different attractions the playground had to offer. Chelsea was chasing Cierra around the jungle gym, only to be blindsided by Calvin, who chose to jump from the slide onto Chelsea's back.

"Oh, you think you can catch me off guard?!" Chelsea laughed and fell into the grass, being cautious of the two kids. She immediately

initiated a tickle-war, and laughter filled the air.

As Chelsea watched the three of them interact, she knew that this was the woman she'd want to spend the rest of her life with. She rummaged through the carrier until she pulled out a ring pop. She didn't have a fancy diamond ring, but she'd replace it soon enough.

"Chels! C'mere bae!"

Chelsea paused her tickle-war and jogged over to Candace with a grin stretching across her face. She placed a hand on her hip, allowing her lungs to collect some much-needed air. "What's up?"

"I love you," Candace began. "I love the way you smile. I love the way you interact with my kids. I love the way you prioritize your naps. No matter what's going on in the world, you're going to take a nap at least once a day."

Chelsea giggled. "You know me, man! I love to sleep."

"I love the way you're able to enjoy life. You've come a long way from the shy girl I met a few years ago. You finally took your life into your own hands and have been prospering ever since. I just love you."

"I love you, too!" Chelsea felt butterflies in her stomach as she looked at the woman she'd grown so fond of over the past several months.

"I want to spend the rest of my life with you. Chelsea Danielle Chisholm, will you marry me?" Candace held out the ring pop with a reassuring smile on her face.

Chelsea scrunched her eyebrows together. "Is this a joke, or are you serious?"

"I'm as serious as a heart attack. I want you to be my wife."

"It would be an honor!" Chelsea allowed Candace to slide the candy onto her finger and smiled brightly.

"I'm going to get you a proper ring, but I just couldn't go another day without asking you to be my woman!"

This brings us back to the present.

"What if I go out there and Candace has changed her mind?" Chelsea let the nerves get the best of her, and she began doubting everything about the day.

"Bitch shut up. This woman has been the most positive aspect of your life. Y'all changed each other for the better. You love her, and she loves you. I know for a fact this finna be y'all happy ending." Tiana reassured her nervous friend. "Plus, I look too damn good for you not to get married today."

Tiana flourished in the medical field. She had even gotten into a relationship with a fellow doctor at her hospital. She was doing what she loved every day and was proud to be in a position to help people.

A knock at the door brought the two women out of their small bubble. Tiana opened the door, and Derrick walked in. "Are you ready?"

Derrick's clothing line had flourished, and he was selling merchandise all over the globe. He had also married Natalie, and the two of them had their ups and downs but prevailed nonetheless.

"Yeah," Chelsea breathed, looking at her reflection in the mirror. "Now or never."

"Well, hurry yo ass up!" Derrick joked, giving his friend a hug and leaving out the door.

A wave of relief overcame her as she walked out into the corridor. She met her father at the entrance to the venue. The wedding was held in a large modern style mansion with Paris in Spring-themed décor. The flower arrangements consisted of white and purple roses. Candace wore a lavender wedding dress while Chelsea wore a white wedding dress. They both had long flowing curls. The family was all seated in rows; the musician began to play the wedding song. As Chelsea was escorted down the aisle by her father, everyone tuned in and gave the wedding party their undivided attention.

The wedding went by smoothly, and then it was time for the vows.

"Chels, you have made me a better woman, a better mother, and a better friend since you came into my life. Our situation was unique; I wasn't even really gay until I met you. It was as if God had made you just for me. You're my soulmate, my other half, my best friend. I can't wait to spend the rest of my life with you." Candace spoke.

Chelsea wiped at her eyes as the emotions began to overwhelm her. "There was a time in my life where I didn't care if I lived or died. There was a time in my life where I wanted to smoke and drink all of my pain away. I was constantly treated like scum. I felt worthless until I met you. You made me feel special; you made me feel loved. I stopped my bad coping mechanisms damn near cold turkey because the feeling you made me feel was better than any drug or drink I could have had."

They finished the ceremony by presenting the rings and their 'I do's. When the ceremony concluded, the fun began. Candace and Chelsea would be spending the rest of their lives together, truly happy.

As for Calvin, he had no intention of settling down any time soon. He enjoyed sex without commitment. He wanted different women every night. He knew he may have a problem and should confront the demons pushing him away from settling down but wasn't ready to admit he had flaws.

"Congratulations," Calvin held out a bottle of champagne as he greeted his ex-wife and ex-lover. "If it weren't for me, this union would have never happened. You're welcome."

"Ni—"

"Nah, baby, let me handle this." Chelsea pressed a kiss to her wife's lips before diverting her attention to the man who was begging for it. "You have to be a delusional ass nigga to think that you're the one responsible for this relationship. I believe that everything happens for a reason. Fate is constantly playing a role in how we go through life. Regardless of your involvement, I wholeheartedly believe that my path would have crossed with Candace's eventually. She was made for me, and you were just the middleman to bring us closer together. You had your chance at happiness, and you blew it because you couldn't control your community dick."

"Now, if all you came to do was be a bitter ex, you can leave and let us enjoy our day," Candace added.

"I ain't mean no disrespect. I'm happy for y'all." Calvin backtracked. "I was just making an observation."

"That no one asked for." Chelsea rolled her eyes.

Calvin shook his head. "I ain't want no drama. I'm a grown-ass man."

"Could have fooled me," Candace mumbled.

"Regardless of how y'all feel about me and the choices I've made, I'm still the father of Candy's kids."

"You're barely that. You let your dick dictate your decisions in life. You're rarely a father figure with your inconsistent ass schedule." Candy shot back.

"This back-and-forth shit is pointless. The divorce is final. The judge created the schedule that best fits the situation. You see your kids on your designated weekends, and the rest of the time, they are well taken care of with Candace and me. Regardless of your unresolved feelings towards us and your divorce, you chose this outcome when you cheated on her for the umpteenth time and contracted fucking gonorrhea. Again, you have bigger things to worry about than what the two of us got going on." Chelsea spoke her final thoughts, and that was that.

"You right." Calvin sighed. "I do wish y'all the best. I'm going to always cherish those nights we spent together."

"Those will be a distant memory. We're secure in our relationship and each other. We won't be spinning the block your way ever again." Candace said her last words and walked away.

For Calvin, he took the little things for granted. He had a one-track mind when it came to how he navigated through the world. If it wasn't his art, he did not care for it. Calvin was in love with his artwork and nothing more. Sex with different women was meaningless to him, but it provided temporary fulfillment of a void he could not fill any other way. He was the perfect addiction for a woman who knew nothing more than temporary satisfaction through sex. He used women for his own gain until they were no longer beneficial to his ego.

For Candace, she was caught in the crossfire of a man who was unable to truly love her but didn't want anyone else to have the opportunity to show her better. She had put herself last for too long. Life was moving faster than she could keep up, and she sadly had wasted a lot of time with a man she knew did not truly love her. She allowed him to cheat on her because she was insecure about herself. It took contracting a sexually transmitted disease to pull her head out of the clouds and bring her back to reality. Settling for subpar love and affection was not how she wanted to spend the rest of her life. Luckily, she was able to find someone who complimented her and provided the missing piece to her complicated puzzle.

For Chelsea, battling depression was her biggest obstacle. Depression is a silent killer that sadly collects lives at an alarming rate. Depression is a battle unique to each soldier fighting it. Some people are able to cope with the sporadic episodes of sadness, anxiety, and a plethora of other symptoms. In Chelsea's case, she often resulted to sex, drugs, and alcohol to numb her body and cloud her mind to fight the battle. She sought out sex to provide companionship and temporary satisfaction with the help of ounces upon ounces of drugs and liters on top of liters of liquor to drown her pain. She'd allowed men to degrade her and use her for years before she finally met someone who saw her as more than a sex object.

Although he was her addiction and she was his muse, the stars did not align for them to be together. Love prevailed for one, and the unresolved inner turmoil continues to guide the other.

The End

Books By This Author

His Little Secret

His Little Secret, Too

Shawty Got A Thing For A Boss

Blessed By Him

Cuffin' In The Summer

Chasing Moon: A Paranormal Romance

Falling For Two Savages

Made in the USA
Coppell, TX
04 July 2025